The Ice Cream Man Cometh

and other stories

Douglas DiNunzio

In a weak moment,
I have written some stories.
(with apologies to Margaret Mitchell)

-- Douglas DiNunzio

for Jean

Author's Preface

When I first considered writing this collection of stories, I was about 70,000 words into a failed novel. Frustrated, and a bit bored, I decided to let the book sit and mellow for a while, even though I knew that trying to resurrect it would be a waste of time. I found myself in the garage going through my filing cabinet, pretty much for the hell of it, and discovered a pair of short stories I'd written maybe ten years ago. They still had the editing marks, corrections, and suggestions made in the margins by my friend and fellow writer, Lawrence Epstein. I started to read them. I could not recall what muse had cajoled or taunted me into writing them back then, but I found myself admiring and enjoying them. It wasn't long, however, before I realized that it really wasn't the stories I was admiring, but rather the form itself. I wondered, given the wasted effort on my novel, if I might try to reconnect with whatever spirit had beguiled me enough to have written those two stories years earlier and see if there were any more of them in me. There might be one or two, but enough for a collection? I wasn't so sure about that. Ray Bradbury once said that a short story writer should write a story every week of the year, the logic being that one could not write fifty-two bad stories in a row. I know now, from trying and failing, that one can indeed write fifty-two bad stories in a row. For there is no less forgiving and no more demanding form of fiction than the short story. Is creating a good one like catching lightning in a bottle? Oh, yes, indeed, and then some.

I was vacationing with my wife in Holland when I first tried to assemble a group of stories. Sometimes I started with a title, and sometimes with the germ of an idea that, more often than not, withered in my harassed imagination and died. Just finding an event, a thought, a memory that could lead to an actual story was a challenge in itself. It was something of a godsend that I was on vacation (*sans* laptop) and could not sit down prematurely and try to write something. The vacation gave the ideas time to simmer and mature. Slowly, I began to assemble a list, and I kept the list in my head until we were back home several weeks later.

It wasn't until I sat down at the computer that I remembered how difficult it was to write a short story. Enough to make me wonder how I could ever have written the two I'd found lingering in my filing cabinet. Were they flukes, aberrations? Had marauding spirits possessed me at the time and then disappeared forever? There is an intensity, a sense of the moment, and a precision with words that no other form of fiction, with the notable exception of poetry, demands. Did I have the skills? The use of one wrong word, or simply too many words, can ruin a piece of short fiction as thoroughly as if the first violin in the New York Philharmonic had played a false note in the middle of a solo. The very thought of writing a short story collection was so intimidating that I decided to consult some of the masters before I went any further. I revisited Poe, Hemingway, Steinbeck, Jack London, O. Henry, Shirley Jackson, H. H. Munro, and Ray Bradbury. Finally, I started to write thirteen more of the stories that I've presented here. I'm already trying to conjure up enough ideas for a second collection. Write a story a week, as Mr. Bradbury suggested? Not possible, but maybe I can come up with at least an idea every week. We'll see.

The stories collected here are not presented in the order that they were written, but rather in a pattern that hopefully will be most pleasing to the reader. It is much like determining the order of songs on a record album: what's going to be on Side One, Band One, for example. I hope that the order in which these stories are presented will help the reader to enjoy them all the more and to see them as parts of an artistic whole, which was kind of the idea. All the stories are set in Brooklyn and environs between the late 1940s and the early 1960s.

-- Douglas DiNunzio

Table of Contents

White Cadillac
by Douglas DiNunzio

Paulie was walking out of Ficorelli's Pharmacy, the Rexall bag with his father's medicine in his hand, when he saw the big white Cadillac convertible parked outside the Sons of Campobasso social club on 18th Avenue. His feet froze him in mid-stride, his eyes ballooned, and his scattered adolescent thoughts coalesced with blinding speed into a reverie as sacred and solemn as prayer.

The Caddy was bone white with a sheen like porcelain. V-8 engine, Synchromesh transmission, sealed beam headlights, front coil springs, hydraulic brakes, slotted disc wheels, safety plate glass. Paulie had memorized the specs and had made pilgrimages to the dealership in Flatbush, continuing his devotions from outside the showroom every time one of the salesmen chased him away. The sticker price for a new '47 Cadillac convertible was more than Paulie's father had earned in a year before the tool-and-die plant in Red Hook pensioned him off for his weak heart.

Paulie approached the Caddy like a priest in the presence of a holy relic. Slowly, he stretched out his hand to touch it, watching his sallow face take shape in its smooth, polished surface, his every feature clear and sharp as in a mirror. His reverie ended when a large, scowling man in the doorway of the social club called to him.

"C'mere, kid," the man said.

"I'm just lookin', mister," said Paulie, taking a step back.

"C'mere anyway," said the man.

Paulie knew about the men who frequented the Sons of Campobasso. They murdered as casually as they combed their hair, wore hundred dollar suits in the middle of the day, and paraded up and down 18th Avenue like kings in their fancy cars. Cars like the big white Cadillac. "Never speak to these men," Paulie's father had warned him countless times, and Paulie's mother would make the sign of the cross.

But Paulie couldn't hear his father's words now, only the sweet siren song of the big white Caddy at the curb. His mind had

1

somehow connected the car to the scowling man in the doorway. He took a small, cautious step toward the man, and then he took another.

Suddenly, he was inside.

There were four men in the small, bare room. One was dressed in a crème-colored suit and matching fedora. Three of his thick fingers sported jeweled rings. One of his front teeth was capped in gold. He had the manner of a don from the old country, and he lounged in his cheap wooden chair as if it were a throne.

"You like the car, kid?" he asked suddenly.

Somehow, Paulie knew that the man would ask about the car. "Yes, sir," Paulie said politely, glancing at the Caddy through the big storefront window, then fixing his eyes on the man again.

"You know who I am?"

"No, sir."

"My name is Santini. Jimmy Santini. I own this street and everybody on it. Whatta you think about that?"

"I guess it's okay."

The man leaned backward as he laughed. "He *guesses* it's okay," he said, turning to the other men. "Hah! The kid *guesses* it's okay. That's pretty good, kid." Santini gave Paulie a longer look. "So, tell me about yourself." His eyes seared through Paulie like blue flame.

Paulie told him what there was to tell. About his pensioned father, his mother and his kid sister, about school and sports and almost making the second string on New Utrecht High's basketball team. Mr. Santini was listening, but not to the words especially. It was more the way you listened to beautiful music with your eyes closed. As Paulie watched him, he thought perhaps it was the music of the words that the mobster heard, the sounds of hope in an honest young man's voice. Sounds not heard, perhaps, in a long, long time. Paulie told him more than he'd planned because Santini seemed to warm to the sounds, and, once or twice, to almost smile. But then, abruptly, he put his hand up and Paulie stopped.

"You really like that car, don't you, kid?"

"Sure, Mr. Santini. It's a swell car. It's a beauty."

"You'd like to drive it around, maybe. Impress all your pals, right?" He paused when Paulie didn't respond and pulled a silver cigarette case from his inside coat pocket. He removed a cigarette, tapped its end against the case, and ignited it. "What would you say if I *gave* you that car?"

"Gave it to me?"

"Gave it."

"*That* car?"

The mobster's eyes narrowed. "That car. You want it, kid?"

Paulie tried to say "yes" so quickly that the word stuck tight in his throat. Santini just smiled and tossed a key ring at Paulie. It had a single General Motors key on it. Paulie stared at the key in his hand and blinked his eyes hard. An inner voice urged him to say, "Gee, thanks, Mr. Santini," bolt out the door, and into the Caddy. But, as always, there was a second voice inside Paulie.

"I only have a junior license, Mr. Santini," Paulie explained. "I'm not allowed to drive by myself."

A cynical smile crossed the face of the mobster. "Listen, kid. Anybody stops you, cops, anybody, you tell 'em that Jimmy Santini gave you this car. You understand?"

"Sure, but I don't know if my Pop..."

"Don't worry about your Pop. You want the car or not?" He leaned back, took a long drag on his cigarette, and exhaled a small gray cloud. The men behind him were smiling.

"Sure. But how come *you* don't want it?"

"Whatta you care?" he said, turning colder and turning his back. Wisps of cigarette smoke drifted over his shoulder.

The sour looks on the other men's faces told Paulie it was time to leave. He did a quick about-face, and again the sight of the white Cadillac overwhelmed him. Rough voices finally propelled him forward. He heard laughter, and he imagined for an instant that this was all just a big joke, that one of the men was already coming for the key. But it was only the laughter of disbelievers.

It occurred to Paulie that he had never started a car like this before. This was no Ford; it had real power under the hood, real gears. The cruel men in the social club were waiting for Paulie to grind those gears like an amateur, like one of those poor dumb nobodies whose lives they determined at will. Nobodies like his father.

Paulie swung the driver's door open, felt the solid weight of it, and slid with unexpected confidence behind the wheel. He placed the Rexall bag beside him, set the choke, slipped the key into the ignition, turned it, and listened to the sweet, smooth roar of the engine. He felt the big wheels move under him, felt the power of eight pounding cylinders moving the Caddy forward like an ocean liner pulling away from a pier. He heard no cruel laughter trailing behind him.

He shifted through second and into third as he approached the corner, downshifted smoothly back into second, turned the big wheels, then shifted into third again. The hard pavement of 83rd Street had become as soft as a cloud under the Caddy's wheels. Paulie was flying, all right. He rolled the Caddy past the line of stucco two-families along 17th Avenue, his proud grin expanding with every block. Children stopped on their bicycles, gossip ladies on front porches halted their discussions, and stickball players in the middle of the street gave way to let him pass. Paulie kept his eyes straight ahead, deep in his reverie, as if no one at all were watching.

By the time he'd reached 17th Avenue and 65th Street, he'd traded the proud grin for a practiced scowl that, he hoped, projected a sense of importance. A scowl like Mr. Santini's. *I could call him Jimmy, now, maybe*, he thought. After another block he was driving the Caddy one-handed, his free arm hanging loosely over the door. *Just the pose for holding a cigarette*, he thought. *If only I had a cigarette.*

When Paulie turned back onto 18th Avenue, he was ready to make an even more impressive pass through the neighborhood. He added to his scowl the casual slouch so many of Santini's hoods had perfected in their long, languid tours along the avenue. He drove by Mr. Anselmo's grocery store, the tailor's shop, the dry cleaners, the luncheonette, the record shop, and the corner newsstand where his father bought the Sunday paper after mass. *Small time people,* he thought. *Nobodies going nowhere.* People on the sidewalk pointed and called Paulie's name. *Invoked* his name. But Paulie paid them no heed. He felt like Julius Caesar parading in his white, eight-cylinder chariot, felt like a king. A true king did not acknowledge the crowd.

As Paulie approached the corner of 18th Avenue and 73rd Street, he saw Annette DeAndrea walking with two of her girlfriends. She was big-busted, tall but not too tall, with wavy brown hair, brown eyes, and smooth olive skin. She was also Billy Stompanato's girl. Billy was the leader of the Vandals, the toughest gang at New Utrecht High School. Annette and Paulie had known each other since grade school. They were friends, but Paulie knew they'd never be anything more. Not as long as handsome punks like Billy Stompanato swaggered through the halls of New Utrecht and made fifteen points a game for the basketball team.

Annette saw the white Cadillac before she saw Paulie behind the wheel. When he pulled the car to the curb and waved, she stopped and stared as if she were looking at someone naked. With that look, Paulie progressed from the skinny, awkward, but pleasant enough boy she sat next to in music class to a potential suitor. All at the speed of light.

"Is that *you*, Paulie?" she asked.

"Nobody else." The confidence in his voice surprised him only briefly, and it didn't desert him when Annette approached the passenger side and leaned on the door of the big Caddy. "Not bad, huh?"

Annette's eyes moved lovingly from the upholstered leather seats to the bright chrome of the dashboard before settling again on Paulie. Her expression turned suddenly grim. "Jesus, Paulie. You didn't *steal* this..."

"Heck, no," Paulie answered with an audacious smile. "Hell, no," was what he'd wanted to say, but the words that the mobsters and punks like Billy Stompanato used with such casual ease did not come naturally. "It's mine," he reassured her. "A gift."

"No kidding?"

"No kidding. You want a ride?"

"Sure," she said as she opened the passenger door and got in. Her girlfriends took only single tentative steps forward before Paulie's fierce, proprietary glare stopped them. Annette had not caught the look, but when the girls glowered, muttered to each other, and stepped back, she understood. "Some gift," she said, smiling, and Paulie smiled back. He put the car in gear and left the girlfriends sputtering jealously in his wake.

Paulie drove several blocks without saying a word. He was back in his mobster's slouch, one hand casually but firmly on the wheel, the other dangling over the door. He switched hands deftly to turn on the radio, switched back, and practiced his mobster scowl again. It was becoming easier now, and with the wind blowing through his tousled hair and the Tommy Dorsey orchestra playing the smoothest of swing, Paulie's confidence soared to new heights.

"You can sit a little closer if you like," he said as he turned onto Linden Boulevard and drove toward Flatbush. Paulie checked the gas gauge. Almost full. Maybe he'd drive to that Caddy showroom where they'd treated him badly. Show them a thing or two. Or maybe Prospect Park or the cemetery. Steal a kiss, or cop a feel, or more. Paulie the make-out artist. Paulie the lover boy. It was amazing what miracles the white Caddy could produce, and in so short a time. There was no end to the miracles. Paulie felt himself transformed. *What if I could go all the way with Annette*, he thought. *I'd need rubbers. Get them from the drugstore. Keep them in the glove box. I'll be a new man then. Maybe I'll even change my name. Paulie's a kid's name. Maybe Paul. Yeah, maybe that. Or Giorgio.*

Annette hadn't moved closer, but Paulie quickly saw the reason. The Rexall bag from the pharmacy was still beside him. "Oh, that," he said, and tossed it casually onto the back seat.

"So," she said, sliding over. "Where'd you get the car?"

"Oh, I'll tell you sometime."

This would be a good time to light a cigarette, he thought. *Next time I'll have cigarettes. And I'll have a fresh hundred in my wallet. She'll see it when I pay for the drinks. We'll have drinks. Up at the Hotel Bossert. I'll get a room. We'll dance the tango. I'll know how.*

"Want a malt?" he asked as they turned onto Flatbush Avenue. Paulie wondered if that might sound too much like the old Paulie, but she signaled agreement with a quick nod. She was changing, too. So much more approachable in these fifteen minutes in the big Caddy than all those long weeks, months, *years* before. The Caddy *was* magical. It would transport him from the cowering, humdrum world of his father to a new universe peopled by giants. He would be among them, the biggest. Bigger even than Mr. Santini.

"It's getting late," Annette said after a half-hour at the malt shop. "I need to be getting home."

"Sure, sure," said Paulie, practicing his nonchalance. *So this is what you do,* he thought. *If you act like you don't care, they have a challenge. They have a reason to want to win you over. You need to play hard to get, just like they do. Why couldn't I figure this out before?*

Paulie noticed that it was indeed getting late, so he cruised one more time around the Soldiers' and Sailors' Memorial Arch just east of Prospect Park and pointed the big Caddy toward Bensonhurst. He didn't waste a word, didn't smile, didn't once turn goofy all the way back. As the breeze played through his hair, he thought, *This is the look. This.* And he felt invincible.

"Thanks, Paulie," Annette said when he dropped her in front of her two-family on 16th Avenue. There was an entirely different luster in her eyes now, one that could pass for admiration. Paulie delighted in it, but with a certain deliberate indifference, as befit his new station in life. Everyone would see him with new eyes now. Not just Annette, but other girls. Women, even, and better than Annette. Much better. So, why settle for Annette? Why put limits on the new Paulie?

"I'll see you at school, then," Annette added after a moment, interrupting his reverie and prompting a scowl that Paulie didn't bother to suppress.

"Sure, maybe."

Annette offered a look of abandonment as Paulie pulled away from the curb. He didn't wave or glance back. He wasn't thinking of Annette anymore, but of Jimmy Santini, his gruff and improbable benefactor. How Paulie felt about the mobster -- how his father had *told* him to feel -- was evolving at a pace almost too quick to comprehend. Jimmy Santini. *Mr.* Santini. Paulie recalled one of his father's maxims: "You have to earn for yourself if you want to be successful in this life. Everything that is good is earned somehow." Mobsters didn't earn, he'd explain. They just took. But hadn't Mr. Santini earned what he had, earned it in harder ways than most people? To be so rich that you could afford to give a new Caddy away without a second thought, that was success. Anybody would tell you that. Anybody but Pop. And what did *he* know, anyway?

Paulie drove five times around New Utrecht High School before he even considered going home. It had taken all that time to make up his mind about the Caddy. It *was* his car, he'd decided, just as Mr. Santini had said. Nobody was taking it away from him. Not his father, not the cops. Nobody.

No lights were on in the brown stucco two-family on 17th Avenue. Paulie pulled the big Caddy to the curb, ran his hand devotedly across the chrome details of the dashboard, and listened to the hum of the engine once more before turning it off. *His* car. Then he remembered the Rexall bag on the back seat. It took a few minutes to find it in the dark.

Paulie didn't see anyone until he saw Mr. Pallerchio, his upstairs neighbor, sitting on the unlit front steps.

"Mr. Pallerchio...?" Paulie began with an undertone of confusion. Mr. Pallerchio was not a stoop sitter, so it was strange to see him there all alone. It was stranger still to see Paulie's house dark. His father would be listening to the ball game, his mother would be sewing, and his sister would be doing her homework.

"Mr. Pallerchio...?"

Mr. Pallerchio lurched up from the steps as if awakened from a bad dream. He rubbed his eyes when he saw Paulie and stepped out under the streetlight.

"Paulie," he said, his voice nearly breaking. "Where have you been?"

"Oh, just around. Where is everybody?"

"Where *were* you, Paulie? Why didn't you come *home*? I told your mother I'd wait for you, but that was *hours* ago. *Hours.* Where *were* you, Paulie? Where *were* you?"

Paulie's eyes fixed on Mr. Pallerchio, and on the fresh tears that ran down Mr. Pallerchio's cheeks. Paulie's breath suddenly left him. His heart pounded in his hollow chest like a drum.

"Your father, he had an attack," said Mr. Pallerchio. "Very bad. They took him to the hospital. Where *were* you, Paulie?"

Where were you?

The Rexall bag dropped from Paulie's hand, but he didn't hear it hit the sidewalk.

It rained during the church service, but the sun came out after the priest's benediction, and the dark earth was almost dry at the cemetery when they lowered Paulie's father down.

Paulie skipped the next three days of school. He wandered through downtown Brooklyn, walked back and forth across the Brooklyn Bridge, sat for hours in the small, triangular park opposite Borough Hall. Finally, he returned to his front stoop, where Mr. Pallerchio had been waiting for him that night. The Caddy was at the curb right where Paulie had parked it. Paulie could not look at it.

After a while, Mr. Lauricella, Paulie's next-door neighbor, came out front with a sledgehammer and a wheelbarrow to break up the old concrete path that led to his back yard. Paulie heard the punishing sound of cast iron on concrete for the next two hours, and when Mr. Lauricella was finished, Paulie rang the doorbell and asked politely if he might borrow the sledgehammer for an hour or so.

"Sure," said Mr. Lauricella, careful not to give Paulie the cold, damning look of the other neighbors. "If you need it, sure, Paulie."

"I'll bring it right back when I'm done," said Paulie, then carefully placed it in the trunk of the white Cadillac.

Mr. Santini was exactly where Paulie had hoped to find him, sitting in the same cheap wooden chair at the Sons of Campobasso. He was wearing a different suit and fedora, but he had the same forbidding look, and the same three hoodlums in his entourage. The front door of the social club was open, and a fan was blowing the sluggish air into the street.

Santini watched the Caddy pull up, watched Paulie get out on the driver's side and carefully shut the door. They made eye contact as Paulie walked with cool deliberation to the back of the car and opened the trunk. Paulie took the sledgehammer out, closed the trunk, and walked slowly to the front of the car. Glaring at the mobster, he lifted the sledge just above his shoulder and held it there. It felt impossibly light, so light that Paulie himself was surprised at how easily he demolished the Caddy's big windshield with a single blow. His eyes darted to Santini, who sat motionless in his chair. Paulie pulled the sledge back again, lifted it above his head, and brought it down on the hood. One of Santini's men started for Paulie, but Santini called him back.

It took three blows to crush the grill and the radiator behind it. Hot water gushed out into the street, and steam rose into the air. Tears began to show on Paulie's face as he took the sledge to the Caddy's doors. Three, four, five blows, and his face was awash in tears. Front quarter panel, rear quarter panel, the trunk, every inch of the Caddy that Santini could see. A crowd had gathered, but Paulie paid them no attention. His eyes saw only the mobster, and the only sound he heard was the hard, crushing thud of iron against steel.

The fury of the attack continued until he grew arm-weary and the long handle of the sledge rested heavily against his leg. Paulie drew labored breaths as he paused, arms limp, sweat mingling with his tears. But he knew that his strength had not failed. It had only changed form. And so it was with his loudest and most fearless voice that he roared at Santini:

"You son of a bitch!...
"You son of a bitch!...
"You son of a bitch!..."

The Ballad of the Sad Hotel
by Douglas DiNunzio

Nick Adams stopped, stood for a moment, and examined the large neon sign that hung over the littered sidewalk. The sign said "Palace Hotel". Nick had been wandering the streets much of the afternoon without an address, searching for it. Now he was finally there, at 315 Bowery. Nick's ride from Trenton had suggested the place because it was cheap, and because it was in Manhattan. Nick had his own reason for wanting to be at the Palace, but he hadn't seen the folly in it yet, and he hadn't known enough about the Bowery when the recommendation was made to decline it. He would know soon enough, and with some discomfort, but he hadn't known back in Trenton, and he still didn't know. Experience was not his middle name.

He had a battered leather suitcase in one hand and a portable Underwood typewriter in a thin metal case in the other. It was high summer in the city, so clothes weren't an issue. He had a couple of T-shirts in the suitcase, a couple pairs of underwear, some socks, pajamas, and the usual toiletries. He was wearing the rest: a frayed summer suit, his only dress shirt, and a broad, loud yellow tie that didn't match the shirt. In his pocket, his leather billfold had exactly seventeen dollars, and there were a few quarters and some smaller change in the one pocket that didn't have a hole in it. He had no plan, except to succeed spectacularly.

The man at the front desk greeted him with a grunt. The low-ceilinged lobby smelled of sweat, tobacco, and indolence. It looked to Nick like the inside of a coffin.

"I'd like a room," said Nick Adams.

"Two bits," grunted the man.

"A day?"

"A day, a night. Twenty-four hours. Whatta you care? You want the room or not?"

Nick wanted the room. It was on the third floor, overlooking the street. There was a rusting metal bed frame along one wall and a thin, slightly soiled mattress rolled on top of it. It had no pillow or sheets, but then the man from the front desk brought them up and dumped them on the threadbare carpet next to the bed.

"The toilet's at the end of the hall," the man said, and quickly disappeared down the corridor. The room was stuffy. Nick opened the window and felt a hot breeze that smelled of animal fat cooking somewhere. He heard the traffic in the street and the dull hum of pedestrians on the sidewalk. He placed his suitcase on the floor. There was a small wooden desk and a metal folding chair in the corner. He set the typewriter case carefully on the desk, unrolled the mattress onto the bed frame, and sat on the bed for a moment, bouncing playfully on the springs. Debauched and dirty as it was, the Palace Hotel was as good a place as any to start.

Another face appeared in the doorway, the face of a rheumy-eyed, tubercular-looking man in his late thirties or early forties. He was smiling, but it was a drunken, feral smile. His large, swollen nose almost glowed.

"*Salve!*" he said. *Quod nomen tibi est?*"

"Excuse me?" said Nick.

"Hello, and what's your name?" asked the man, who was now inside the room and walking briskly toward the open window. Nick answered, his brow forming tight knots of confusion and curiosity. The man stopped at Nick's typewriter case and screwed up his face.

"Whatever do you keep in there?" he asked. "It's too small for a Tommy gun."

"It's a typewriter," said Nick.

"What you need a typewriter for?"

"I'm a writer," said Nick.

"A *writer?*"

"Yes."

"Ah! You say you're a writer, but I think maybe you're only a typist," the man said, his smile growing wider. "*Timebunt angeli stulti irruitis in conculationem.*"

"I don't quite understand," said Nick.

"Don't worry. It's not necessary here. You hungry, Old Sport? They've got a reasonable excuse for a restaurant downstairs."

Nick had seen it. The Palace Restaurant Bar and Grill. "I could eat some dinner," he said.

"You'd better bring that typing machine with you," the man said. "There's no locks on these doors, and there's a pawn shop right around the corner. *Mox pecunia diviserunt stulto.* And that goes for fools and their typewriters, too."

They sat at a small, round table by the front window. A cop was passing by on the sidewalk, absently twirling his nightstick. Nick set the typewriter case on the floor between his legs, keeping it in close contact with his knees.

"Name's Kibbee," said the man. "Guy Kibbee, like the actor. You ever seen *Mr. Smith Goes to Washington*? He's in that one. I met him once, on Market Street in San Francisco, but that's another story."

"I see," said Nick, without enthusiasm.

"The stew's not too bad here, but I'd stay away from the clam chowder if I were you. Guy last week got ptomaine eating the chowder. *Caveat emptor,* and all that."

"And what are *you* doing here?" asked Nick.

"*Here* here?"

"At this hotel. At the Palace. And you don't have to explain it in Latin this time."

"You understand Latin?" asked Kibbee.

"A little. Tenth grade."

"*Scire modicum periculosum.*"

"You could say that," said Nick. The waiter wandered over. "I'll have the stew," said Nick. "And a Coke."

"Not hungry," said Kibbee to the waiter, "but I'll have a drink. Two fingers of your best rot-gut, if you don't mind." He coughed and gave Nick a surreptitious look. "The doctors suggest that I might have a touch of TB," he said with a grin. "But then again, I might not. So, what do you want to write about?"

"Life," said Nick, and Kibbee laughed.

"*Life?*" Kibbee said with some indignation. "Hell, why don't you write about porcupines, or apple jelly? Jesus! *Life?*"

"You still haven't told me why you're here," said Nick with rising irritation.

"No, I haven't, have I?"

"If you can't answer any of my questions, you might at least try answering some of your own."

"*Touché, mon ami.* You cut me to the quick. I am, in fact, a failed writer of some substance. A novelist, a poet. A *raconteur* of sorts. I even stayed at the Chelsea Hotel when Tom Wolfe was there. You ever hear of him? Not in tenth grade, I imagine. Well, I was there when he was there. On the same damn floor, even. Fifteen years ago. What do you think about that? I was there. And now I'm here. That's porcupines for you. That's real apple jelly."

The waiter shambled over with Kibbee's drink and placed it in front of him. Nick scowled at the waiter. "Okay, okay," the waiter said. "The stew's coming."

"And a Coke," Nick reminded him. "With ice."

"So, I'm here. And now *you're* here, too," said Kibbee with a wry, caustic smile. "On your way up, you imagine, just as I'm on my way down. Well, I'm past down, actually. Well past that sad marker. Oh, I don't mean to discourage you, Old Sport. Every dog should have his day, or the sweet illusion of one. I had mine, you've got yours. Life and porcupines, they go on, my friend. With us or without us. Ah, but I talk too much."

"Can I pay for your drink?" Nick asked.

"You can, but you may not. Good grammar, that. You need good grammar to be a writer, that's what I think. Unless you're ol' Bill Faulkner, of course. You know about him?"

"Of course."

"*The Sound and the Fury.* Never understood a word of it. No decent grammar at all in it."

"I don't mind paying for your drink," said Nick.

"You're changing the subject," said Kibbee. "But it's excusable, given your lack of experience and, even more, your lack of failure.

You haven't failed yet, have you? You haven't even started to fail. You haven't even started *thinking* about failure. Let me guess: you've got a ream of typing paper in that typewriter case between your knees, and you haven't so much as typed out a title for whatever *magnum opus* you're planning. Well, have you, Sport? What have you done in the world? Where have you been? You figured you'd just come to some cheap hotel like this one, for writer's ambiance or whatever, do a little fashionable slumming, and start churning out peerless prose off the top of your gifted head? Is that what you thought?"

The waiter shambled over with the stew and Coca-Cola, and Kibbee went silent, sipping his liquor and glaring across the table. Nick ate without pleasure. He wanted to go up to his room and close the door, but he thought that Kibbee would just follow him with more taunts and challenges. Some time passed. Nick was almost done with his stew. His glass of Coke was empty.

"There was a guy here a month ago," said Kibbee. "He wanted to be a writer, like you. Like me. Tried to shoot himself in the head. Didn't even die. Can you believe it? Just creased his thick skull with a .45. Now, there's failure for you. A perfectly good instrument of destruction, and he couldn't even kill himself. That kind of stuff goes on here at the Palace all the time."

"I'd like to go up to my room now," said Nick in a hollow voice.

"Sure, sure. Go right ahead. *Absentia cor amantius facit.*"

"I'll see you tomorrow, maybe."

"If you hear a gunshot from down the hall, that'll be me. And I won't miss." He paused a moment, smiled and said, "Just kidding, Old Sport. I'm past suicide, too. Slow and steady self-destruction, that's plenty good enough for me these days. Did you catch the alliteration there? *Slow and steady self-destruction?* Good, huh? But then, I was a poet once."

"Good night," said Nick, and Kibbee lifted his glass of rot-gut in a sardonic salute.

Nick tucked the typewriter case under his arm and went slowly up to his room. It was cooler now, but the breeze felt good, so he left the window open. He opened the case, placed the Underwood portable on the desk, and tore open the ream of paper. He slid a clean sheet under the roller, advanced the sheet, set the carriage, and stared at the empty page. It seemed to stare back at him in undisguised contempt, and once again it issued him a challenge that had as yet gone unanswered. No, not even a title, he thought. Not even that much. Nothing. Less than nothing.

He slept fitfully. Each time he awoke, he told himself that he did not want to see Kibbee anymore. He even thought of moving to the Lanier, a good ten blocks down from the Palace. The rooms cost the same, and there was a cheap restaurant next door called Fuerst Bros., where he could take his meals in peace. Kibbee had been right about one thing, though. Nick had come to the Palace Hotel to play a part -- the noble, starving artist achieving greatness in his lonely garret. It had been a foolish idea, an infantile idea, and an embarrassment. In the morning, he would pack up his suitcase and his typewriter and take his leave of the Palace Hotel. Then he would return to Trenton, where he could lick his wounds in private.

It rained hard during the night. In the early morning, Nick got out of bed to close the window, and when he did, he happened to look down at the sidewalk. There was a man there, lying face up, right under Nick's window, three floors down. The man's tan summer suit was stained red in several places, and his eyes were open. His round head shone like the moon under the streetlight.

Nick took the steps two at a time. When he reached the lobby, Kibbee and the desk clerk were standing solemnly at the entrance to the Palace Hotel.

"Go on back upstairs, Old Sport," said Kibbee. "We've got it covered down here. *Mortem omnibus nobis arridere,* or something to that effect."

But Nick could not resist the temptation to stare at the corpse. He had never seen a dead body before. Not one like this, anyway. Never like this. Only at the funeral home in Trenton. Only in that most artificial of places. A shadow crossed the corpse, and a beat cop in a raincoat briefly came into view before disappearing again.

"What happened?" Nick asked, but the cop didn't answer. Nick stared again at the corpse, and then at the two men.

"Tell you later, Old Sport," said Kibbee. "Go on back upstairs."

He found Kibbee at the bar and grill having breakfast just after eight that morning. The place was half-full. Or half-empty.

"Try the pancakes, Old Sport," said Kibbee with an almost pleasant smile. "The batter's probably two days old, but they're only two bits a stack."

Nick sat down. "Are you going to tell me now?"

"Sorry about dinner last night," said Kibbee. "I sort of popped my cork at you. Bad form. *Mea culpa, mea culpa.*"

"You know what I mean," said Nick.

"Oh, *that.* Happens all the time here at the Palace."

"Who was he?"

"Just a gunsel. Worked for the mobster, Anastasia, until he did something stupid or disloyal enough to merit a chest full of bullets. Albert's wolves were after him. Too bad. Not a bad sort of guy, for a gunsel."

"You knew him?"

"Hell, he lived right here, Old Sport. Maybe that's why they dumped him here. He was hiding out, but they found him. He had the room right under yours. I hadn't seen him for a couple of days, so I was kind of hoping he'd gotten away. He told me once he was from Philly. Wanted to go back to Philly. Won't get there now."

"Jesus," said Nick, and went pale.

"You okay?" asked Kibbee.

"I guess."

"Not a pretty sight, was it?"

"No."

"See that kind of thing all the time here. Well, other than that, how was your first night at the Palace, Old Sport? Started writing that *magnum opus* yet?"

"I'm checking out this morning," said Nick. "I'm going back to Trenton."

"Your folks, they live there? In Trenton?"

"Yes."

"Nice and clean in Trenton, I suppose. And quiet. Never been there myself. Been a lot of places, but Trenton's not one of 'em. A well-kept community, no doubt."

"It's okay."

"*Vita deformis esse, sed est vita.* You want the translation, Old Sport?"

"No, thanks," said Nick, and stood up so he could say goodbye from a distance.

Kibbee's rheumy eyes suddenly bore in on him. "You want to write about *life*, Old Sport? If you do, stay right here. You'll find plenty of it." Kibbee turned eagerly in his chair and pointed. "You see that old baldy there at the end of the bar? That man can open a can of beer with his front teeth. I've seen him do it. And that bushy-haired guy over in the corner, the one with the newspaper? Claims he's a Republican turned anarchist. He's got a PhD in something or other. Speaks more languages than I do. And the old guy across the hall from you -- he makes birdcages out of Popsicle sticks. Can you believe that? Got another who forges fine art, mostly Dali. We got a circus midget who speaks in tongues and a hophead who used to make stag movies. We got a colored here, too, just down the hall from me. Played ball with Cool Papa Bell back in the Negro League. We also got us a crazy Cuban, old as dirt, claims he fired pot shots at Teddy Roosevelt up on San Juan Hill. And then there's me, of course. I've got some swell stories to tell about ol' Tom Wolfe. I might even share some with you, if provoked. As for the colorful residents of this fine hotel, I'll take you around for an invite, if you like."

The waiter shambled over. "What're you having, kid?"

But Nick didn't hear him. He stopped in the lobby only long enough to give the desk clerk a shiny quarter and a smile, then raced the three floors up to his room. His typewriter was just where he'd left it. Quickly he sat down in the folding chair and typed: *My Happy Life at the Sad Hotel*, by Nicholas Adams.

And he went straight back to Kibbee.

The Actor
by Douglas DiNunzio

Every second Saturday, the women of 83rd Street took up a fruit and vegetable collection. Mrs. Apicella and Mrs. Fazio went around to each house with bushel baskets just after breakfast and loaded up for the day: souring tomatoes, rotting leaf lettuce, molding green peppers. Anything that would splatter on impact.

Soon they would take their posts at the corners of 16th and 17th Avenues, place their bushel baskets in the hot summer sun, and wait for Old Mr. Grassi's only daughter Maria and her Polack husband Howard to arrive by taxicab in early afternoon.

Maria and Howard had learned never to use their own vehicle for the bi-weekly visits. As soggy as that old produce was, it could still make a dent if thrown with vigor, and it was almost impossible to wash off once it dried. So, as always, they parked their new Buick Roadmaster in downtown Brooklyn and took an expendable cab to 83rd Street.

Where the neighborhood waited in ambush.

Old Mr. Grassi himself took no interest in his neighbors' grim preparations. Lucy, his sweet wife of fifty years, had passed away the previous winter, and he'd stopped caring about anything at all after that. He didn't even care when Maria and Howard moved away to New Jersey the following spring. He cared so little that it could almost be mistaken for forgiveness. But the women of 83rd Street were neither apathetic nor forgiving. Maria and Howard had committed the most heinous form of patricide, which is abandonment. Their punishment, their special penance, was to be scourged every second Saturday with whatever spoiled produce the neighbors could find to throw at them.

At high noon, Mrs. Ettore and Mrs. Buono took their accustomed posts at 15th and 18th Avenues, armed with cowbells. Perched high on the roofs of apartment houses, one or the other would send the alarm: a single clang if Maria and Howard took their usual northern route down New Utrecht Avenue, two if they tried a more surreptitious approach from Dyker Heights, three if they made a cowardly end run up from Bath Beach.

It was not the lookout ladies, however, but Mrs. D'Amato, glancing out her own kitchen window, who actually set the day's events in motion.

"Look at that," she said to Mrs. Panetta, pointing at the flat roof of Old Mr. Grassi's house.

"Look at *what*?"

"Up there, look! Old Mr. Grassi's on his roof."

"So? He's always up there."

"But look, he's carrying something. What's he carrying? An end table?"

"I can't see," said Mrs. Panetta. "I don't have my glasses."

"It is! It's an end table! *Mario!*"

Her burly, scowling, T-shirted husband appeared. "*What?*"

"Look up there at Old Mr. Grassi's. What's going on?"

"How the hell should I know?"

"*Look*, for crying out loud! There, on his roof. What's he *doing*?"

Mario squinted at the roof, then winced as if he felt a sudden pain. "He's got his furniture up there. Jesus! He's got *all* his furniture up there."

"And look! There's the Victrola!"

Old Mr. Grassi lumbered across the roof and carefully placed the Victrola at the edge.

"Mrs. Panetta!" Mrs. Bonafiglio shouted from the street. "Mr. Grassi's gone crazy! He's boarded up his house, and all his furniture is on the roof! What's going on?"

Before Mrs. Panetta could answer, the old Edison cylinder on Old Mr. Grassi's Victrola began to turn, and the music started. Mrs. D'Amato made a quick sign of the cross. "Oh, my God!" she said. "He's playing *Aida*."

"Jesus, Mary, and Joseph!" shouted Mrs. D'Amato's husband, and bolted for the street.

It wasn't unusual for Old Mr. Grassi to set his Victrola on the roof in summer. He often sat up there and listened to those scratchy old Edison cylinders, his eyes half-closed, an iced tea in his large, pale, bony hand, a cool breeze from Jamaica Bay playing through his fine, white, thinning hair. He serenaded the street hour after hour: *Rigoletto, Il Trovatore, La Boheme, La Traviata.* And when he accompanied the music with his own smooth baritone, the neighborhood felt almost blessed.

But *Aida* was different.

"So, what's so special about *Aida*?" Mr. D'Amato had once been foolish enough to ask.

"What's so *special*?!"

"Yeah. I don't get it."

"You're a moron, Mario. *Imbecille!*"

"I still don't get it."

"*Aida*, stupid. The *story*. Rhadames, the king's general, he's so much in love with the princess that he goes into the tomb with her."

"So?"

"Into the *tomb* with her."

"I still don't get it."

"Lucy's in the *ground*, half-wit."

"So, he's depressed again?"

"Brilliant."

The first piece of Old Mr. Grassi's furniture, a three-drawer dresser, sailed off the roof at 12:17 pm, only moments before Maria's and Howard's cab pulled up unheralded at the curb. Nobody had sounded the alarm, nobody had pelted the cab with rotting fruits or vegetables. They were all clustered around Old Mr. Grassi's house, their worried eyes turned upward. Even when the cabbie brashly beeped his horn to clear a path to the curb, not a soul on 83rd Street seemed to notice.

Old Mr. Grassi was propping a nightstand at the edge of the roof when Mr. D'Amato shouted up, "No, no, Mr. Grassi. Please, not the nightstand!" But the old man paid no heed. He tipped it casually over the edge, and, without even waiting to watch it shatter on his front walk, went to get something else.

Mrs. Panetta's husband raced up to Mrs. D'Amato's in time to see a second nightstand shatter on the walk.

"He's got the doors and windows locked, but we might get in through a cellar window and work our way up," Mr. Panetta explained as though he were describing a military operation. Mr. Panetta had been with the 82nd Airborne in the war, so he knew a thing or two about house breaking.

"No, no, Mr. Grassi!" Mr. D'Amato shouted up again. "Not the armchair! It's such a nice piece! Think what you could do with it!" But over it went, and again, Old Mr. Grassi trundled out of sight.

"Talking to him's not gonna work," said Mr. D'Amato glumly. "We've got to get up there."

"Even if we get to the roof, how we gonna stop him from jumpin'?"

"We'll grab him."

"Are you kidding? He's as strong as an ox. He'll take us both with him."

It was true. Back in the old country, Old Mr. Grassi had been a mounted policeman, a proud, one might even say vainglorious, member of the *carabinieri*. Even in his mid-seventies, he still had the stature and strength of a soldier. Only his mind now seemed to fail him.

"Papa, you stop this silliness," Old Mr. Grassi's daughter shouted, and her fat Polack husband Howard echoed her. Old Mr. Grassi couldn't hear either of them over *Aida*, but the neighbors could. Small hissing noises escaped from the hostile crowd, enough to make Howard nudge his wife nervously back to the cab. But the pariahs were already surrounded by a phalanx of irate neighbors and were going nowhere.

When Old Mr. Grassi paused from his demented labors long enough to change cylinders on the old Edison machine, Mr. D'Amato called up to him again. Old Mr. Grassi responded by tossing a large, upholstered armchair off the roof, scattering everyone as it crashed to the sidewalk.

"Okay, mister wise guy," said Mrs. Panetta to Mr. D'Amato. "Got any other big ideas?"

It was the widow lady, Old Mrs. Brunotelli, who had the answer. "You can't *make* him come down. You have to trick him," she said.

"And how are we supposed to do that?"

"His mother."

"His *mother*? She's been dead for twenty-five years!"

"Have you ever seen a full-grown man more attached to his mother?" argued Old Mrs. Brunotelli. "A regular mama's boy he was, even after he married Lucy. 'Yes, Mama. No, Mama. Thank you, Mama. Whatever you say, Mama.' Remember?"

Mr. D'Amato's face was suddenly awash with confusion. "You're tellin' us you're gonna get a dead woman out of her grave so she can get Old Mr. Grassi off his roof?"

"Of course not," said Old Mrs. Brunotelli. "But we've got to make him *think* it's his mother up there."

"And how do we do that?"

"The actor boy down the street."

"*Who*?"

"Mrs. Dellasandro's son. What's his name?"

"Danny?"

"Exactly."

"You're jokin'."

"Not at all," said Mrs. Brunotelli. "All we have to do is put a dress and a wig on him and have him talk like Old Mr. Grassi's mother. The old man's so addle-headed, he'll probably believe it."

"Danny Dellasandro ain't no actor," grumbled Mr. D'Amato.

"Of course he is, " said Old Mrs. Brunotelli. "Why, he even went to acting school."

"With all due respect, Mrs. Brunotelli, that don't make him an actor. He's been to -- what -- twenty, thirty, auditions? Not *one* single job did he land. Not *one*. He even muffed that tv soap commercial that only had three words in it."

Old Mr. Grassi's love seat began its plunge toward the crowded front walk, and the spectators scattered again.

"No offense, Mrs. Brunotelli," Mr. D'Amato continued, "but Danny Dellasandro couldn't act his way out of a candy wrapper. That's why he's twenty-five years old, ain't married, and is still livin' at home. He's a loser."

"So, you got a better idea, Einstein?" argued Mrs. D'Amato, sidling up to Old Mrs. Brunotelli and offering her husband a sour face. "When that last piece of furniture goes over the edge, Old Mr. Grassi's goin' over next. We got no other choices. Well?"

Mr. D'Amato frowned and scratched his head.

"Well?"

"I'm thinkin'," said Mr. D'Amato.

"We don't have time to hire Clark Gable or Humphrey Bogart," his wife insisted. "It's gotta be the Dellasandro kid."

"We could call the cops. They got a net."

"And haul the old man off to Bellevue? To the nuthouse?"

"Okay, okay, we'll try the kid, but if you ask me, it's gonna be a big waste of everybody's time."

Danny Dellasandro had been watching the commotion from his bedroom window, taking a break from organizing his Spider Man comics. Danny did a lot of street watching nowadays, especially since that last disastrous audition for the soap commercial. Not enough charisma, plus poor voice projection. That's what the unsympathetic station manager had told him when he showed Danny to the door. It was what they all said, but the voice coach at the acting school had said it best: "You've got no confidence, kid, and it shows."

"What's going on, Danny?" his mother asked as she came into the room.

"Old Mr. Grassi," he answered. "He's up on his roof throwin' stuff."

"You going to play checkers with him today?"

"I was, but..."

"You sure it's a healthy thing, spending so much time with him, playing checkers all the time?"

"He's a nice old man, Mama. And he's lonely. He needs somebody to keep him company."

"You should be going out with some girls, Danny. Some nice girls from the neighborhood. That's the company you should keep."

There was a knock at the door. Danny went to answer it, and Mr. Panetta and Mr. D'Amato entered.

"We've got an acting job for you," said Mr. Panetta.

"It doesn't pay," said Mr. D'Amato, but Danny went along with them anyway.

Mrs. D'Amato and Old Mrs. Brunotelli were already sizing Danny up for a print dress when they heard another piece of furniture shatter on the walk in front of Old Mr. Grassi's house.

"That was a big one," observed Mrs. Panetta. "Sounded like a full chest o' drawers, or maybe a table."

"If he's tossing the big stuff, he'll be goin' over himself pretty soon," cautioned Mrs. D'Amato. "We got to hurry with this dress. Sorry I got no wig, Danny. Old Mr. Grassi's mother certainly didn't have no crew cut, so that could be a problem. You're gonna have to pull this off with the dress alone."

"And your voice," said Mrs. Panetta. "Can you do her voice?"

"I'll try," Danny said, looking very pale, the timbre of his voice quaking, as if he had not quite arrived at puberty.

"Danny wasn't even born when Old Mr. Grassi's mother died," Mrs. D'Amato complained. "How's he s'posed to know what she sounded like?"

"Well, he just better get it right, that's all. You just better get it right, kid."

"I'll sure try, Mrs. Panetta," said Danny, but his mouth had gone so dry that his answer was barely more than a whisper.

"You'll do fine," said Old Mrs. Brunotelli.

Old Mr. Grassi had a fake leather recliner chair perched at the edge when they snuck Danny in through a cellar window. Mr. Panetta was too fat to get in that way, so Danny let him in through the storm door, and Mrs. Panetta, Old Mrs. Brunotelli, and Mrs. D'Amato followed.

"We've got to hurry," said Mrs. Panetta. "He could go over any minute now," and Mrs. D'Amato made a hurried sign of the cross.

Old Mr. Grassi's house was a two-story stucco like every other house on the block. It was small and cramped, but without any furniture it looked bigger, almost roomy inside. So many memories here for a place that suddenly appeared unlived-in and barren. It was all so very sad when it wasn't terrifying. If he hadn't liked Old Mr. Grassi so much, and if Mr. Panetta hadn't been right on his heels, Danny would already have fled the place in panic, back to his comic book collection and his daytime television programs, never to show his cowardly face on 83rd Street again.

"Come on!" said Mrs. Panetta when the others joined Danny in gawking at all the empty space. "Hurry up!"

Old Mr. Grassi was at the very edge of the roof with a coffee table lifted effortlessly over his head when they arrived. His back was to them, and although the door to the roof creaked when they pushed it open, he didn't seem to notice. "All right, Danny," Mrs. D'Amato whispered. "Go on out there now. We're going to hide behind this door. You just make sure he comes this way, so we can grab him and get him inside. You understand?"

Danny nodded once, his eyes bulging with fear, his Adam's apple doing double-time pushups inside his throat.

"You've *got* to get him over here," said Mrs. D'Amato.

"You'd better not fail," warned Mr. Panetta.

"You can do it, Danny," said Old Mrs. Brunotelli. "Just remember how much you like that old man out there."

Danny adjusted his dress and waited awkwardly while Mr. Panetta closed the door behind him. It was like being pushed into the Roman Coliseum where a dozen hungry lions were waiting. His stomach started doing somersaults to match the pushups his

Adam's apple was still doing, and his legs began to feel like the thinnest of rubber bands. *What the hell am I doing here?* he thought. *I can't do this! I can't do this!"*

Old Mr. Grassi had just tossed the last kitchen chair into the wild blue. He had nothing left to toss but himself. Even *Aida* seemed finished. The needle was making a dull scratching sound against the end of the cylinder as Old Mr. Grassi peered longingly at the ground below. He teetered for a moment, then steadied himself.

"Come on!" Mr. Panetta whispered harshly as Danny still had not moved a step forward. "Hurry it up, already!"

Danny stared at Old Mr. Grassi, gritted his teeth, and tried to keep his knees from buckling. He remembered how much he truly, truly, liked the old man, how much he enjoyed the old man's company, how much he looked forward to their friendly checker competitions every afternoon. And he remembered what Old Mrs. Brunotelli had told him about Old Mr. Grassi's mother while Mrs. D'Amato had fitted Danny for the dress. He knew also there was no one in the world who could save the old man now but him. If his acting wasn't up to snuff, the old man would die.

"Alphonso!" Danny shouted suddenly across the roof. It was the name by which Old Mr. Grassi's mother had always called her eldest son, and he probably hadn't heard it spoken that way in the twenty-five years since her death. *Old Mr. Grassi.* Danny thought it was strange that nobody ever seemed to call old people by their given names. Old Mr. Grassi and Old Mrs. Brunotelli, not Alphonso or Laura. Danny wondered what it would feel like when he was old enough to be known as Old Mr. Dellasandro. If he were lucky, truly lucky, he wouldn't ever live that long.

"Alphonso!" Danny shouted again. "What are you doing up on this roof? How many times do I have to tell you it's dangerous up here?"

Old Mr. Grassi turned slowly around. He looked confused, like he was trying to find a ghost inside a cloud.

"Where is your brother, Alphonso?" scolded Danny. "Where is Gaetano?" The voice sounded so good, so true, so absolutely unlike Danny that it took him quite by surprise. He *was* the woman. The woman's robust spirit inhabited him, breathed an actor's life into him, spurred him on. As the old man stared back in confusion, Danny scowled and put his hands on his hips, just as Old Mrs. Brunotelli had taught him to do, and just as Old Mr. Grassi's mother had done when Old Mr. Grassi was still a boy. "Where is your brother?" scolded Danny, every word searing with parental scorn. He *was* the woman. He *was*.

Somewhere in that part of his mind that lived only in the past now, Old Mr. Grassi recognized the voice, remembered the one who had been dead for so many years. "He's at school, Mama," he answered meekly. "He's still at school."

"That's what *you* say. Teacher says he plays hooky. All day long. You play hooky, too?"

"No, Mama," said Old Mr. Grassi.

"Maybe you go whoring again, maybe you go with the sluts, hah? You want to kill your mother with heartbreak? Is that what you want?"

"No, Mama," sobbed Old Mr. Grassi.

"How many times I have to tell you these things?"

"I'm sorry, Mama. I'm...sorry."

"I'll give you *one* minute to get downstairs and wash for dinner. If your brother's not home in five, he's gonna get the strap."

Without hesitation, Old Mr. Grassi walked toward Danny, put his head on Danny's shoulder, and cried like a baby. As the onlookers in the street cheered, Mrs. D'Amato met Danny at the door and led Old Mr. Grassi downstairs to the kitchen, where a smiling Old Mrs. Brunotelli offered to take care of him for a while. Mr. Panetta and Mrs. D'Amato, beaming their own proud smiles, escorted Danny to the front stoop, where Mr. Panetta and Mr. D'Amato hoisted him onto their strong shoulders and carried him around 83rd Street in triumph. Maria and Chuck departed in the taxi through a hail of rotting produce, and the neighborhood erupted with the sounds of a full-scale celebration.

In his empty kitchen, Old Mr. Grassi was pouring *annisette* into a pair of shot glasses. He smiled and offered one to Old Mrs. Brunotelli.

"Well," he said. "Didn't I tell you?"

"You were right, Alphonso. You were absolutely right."

"All the boy needed was a little..."

"Confidence."

"Exactly."

"It worked perfectly."

"It *did*, didn't it?"

"You shouldn't have stood so close to the edge, though."

"Was I too close?"

"Yes. You had me worried. And the furniture!"

"Never cared for it much. It was Lucy's mother's set. Maybe we could go downtown tomorrow, replace every stick of it with Danish Modern. You like Danish Modern?"

"If you do."

"Maybe even pick up one of those new stereo-phonic players while we're at it. A really good one. I'm tired of listening to that old Victrola."

"And who's going to pay for all this?"

"My worthless daughter and her half-wit Polack husband, that's who."

"Perfect," said Old Mrs. Brunotelli.

"I thought so."

"All's well that ends well."

"Well, isn't that the truth."

Old Mr. Grassi smiled the way he used to smile at Lucy when they first courted. "To the actor!" he said, raising his shot glass.

"*Actors*," said Old Mrs. Brunotelli.

"*Salut!*"

Tenacity
by Douglas DiNunzio

Charlie Thayer shivered in the dark at the end of an alley between a shoe repair and a Chinese laundry in Brownsville. The rain was cold and hard, harder than Charlie was used to, and he wasn't dressed for it. He hadn't had the *time* to dress for it, and anyway, he wasn't used to this kind of outdoor life. He had always preferred the smooth, warm interiors of Manhattan clubs and restaurants to this feral harshness. It had been raining hard like this for several hours, and the alley was starting to flood. It had originally been paved with red brick, but there was a thin layer of crumbling asphalt over most of it now. There was no light in the alley, but the streetlight on Pitkin Avenue cast a soft, shimmering, yellowish glow halfway to the place where Charlie was standing. Water from the flat roof of the building that housed the laundry was cascading a few feet away, splashing loud enough on the brick and asphalt to drown out the traffic noises on Pitkin Avenue. There was no exit at the end of the alley, and that worried Charlie. What if she didn't come? What if his sweet Rosie didn't come? What if *they* came instead? He'd called her almost an hour ago from the phone booth on the corner. Plenty of time to get to the bank and then get herself here. But what if *they* came instead? And what was it all about anyway? Why did they want to kill him, for crying out loud? For *that*? For one lousy, pathetic performance at the club?

Charlie pulled the collar of his raincoat tighter around his neck. A thin stream of water ran off the peak of his fedora and splashed against the legs of his pants, long since soaked through. Where the hell *was* Rosie anyway? Another five minutes of this waiting, this supreme discomfort, and he'd have to find another alley, another phone booth, and try her again. She *had* to come. She *had* to. Just bring the money. Just enough to get him out of town for a while, until everybody calmed down and things got back to normal. Then he would apologize, if necessary. Beg, if necessary.

He just needed some time and a place of refuge, a place to get away to. She *had* to come.

A Yellow cab pulled up to the curb on Pitkin Avenue, and Charlie tensed for a moment, just a moment, until he knew it was Rosie with that transparent umbrella she always carried rain or shine, because she liked to carry it. She stood quite still on the sidewalk as the cab pulled away, not moving until she heard Charlie's weak, muffled voice calling from the alley. She was not a pretty girl, or talented. He could always have done better, but she was the only real certainty in his life these past few hard years, and she loved him, and that was enough for both of them, for Charlie had his own share of imperfections.

Rosie covered them both with the transparent umbrella and hugged him tightly. There was both love and fear in her eyes, but no tears.

"Charlie!" she said just over the sound of the rain. "Oh, Charlie!"

"Did you bring the money, babe?" he asked. "Did you bring it?"

"A hundred and twenty-seven dollars," she said, handing him the roll of bills. "It's all I had in savings. I hope it's enough. Oh, Charlie, Charlie! Why?"

"Honest to God, Rosie, I don't know."

"You don't *know*?"

"Honest to God, I don't. At least, I don't remember."

"The mobster's wife. At the club. You don't remember *her*? Alberto Scarpetti's wife, and you don't *remember*?"

"I was drunk."

"You're always drunk, Charlie."

"No. Not always."

"They were at the front table. You don't remember that?"

"Well, maybe..."

"You *insulted* her. You made *jokes* about her. *Crude* jokes. *Right from the stage!* What in God's name were you thinking?"

"I don't know. I wasn't... I mean..."

"And then you *kept* doing it. Even after you saw how angry he was. Why?"

"I told you, I don't know. I was drunk."

"That's not an excuse, Charlie."

"Damn it," said Charlie. "Damn it all to hell."

"Do you remember the thug who came to your dressing room after the show? Do you remember *him*? Do you remember what he *said*?"

"He said that I wasn't funny."

"No. He said that *Mr. Scarpetti* didn't think you were funny."

"All right, all right."

"And later, the manager of the club, after you'd sobered up. Do you remember what *he* told you?"

"That I should get out of town."

"And what else?"

"That I was through at the club."

"Oh, Charlie. Why?"

"It's the drink, Rosie. The booze. I can't handle the booze any more. That's why. And that's all, really. But why do they want to kill me? For a couple of bad jokes? I can apologize. I can do that. Why won't they *let* me?"

"It's not just the drink, Charlie. It's something else with you. Something more."

"What, then?"

"Jeez, Charlie. Can't *you* see it? It's like you have a death wish or something. Can't you tell a joke without insulting everybody in the audience? A dirty joke, even, is better than that. And a mobster's *wife*, for crying out loud. Oh, Charlie. *Why?*"

Charlie felt the full weight of his body sag against the wet wall, his short, chubby legs turning to rubber. "I just can't seem to take hold, Rosie. Things just seem to slip away from me, or I slip away from them. I try to hold on, I really do, but then I screw up and I start to slip away all over again. I've *got* to take hold someplace, sometime. If I could just *take hold...*"

"And what about now? What about *this* time?"

"This time I gotta run."

"That's not taking hold, Charlie."

"Jesus, they're trying to *kill* me, Rosie. For some bad jokes. For some insults, too, maybe, okay, but..."

"What are you going to do?"

"My brother Benny's coming. He's gonna drive me out to the Island. I can catch the ferry at Orient Point and maybe hole up in Connecticut for a while. It'll be good for me. Give me a chance to quit the booze, maybe work up some new routines. Give me a little time to get straightened out with Mr. Scarpetti. Then I can come back, *really* come back, take hold, start fresh."

Rosie gave him that look again, the one that had pity but no love in it. "You're expecting help from *Benny*? He's a *junkie*, Charlie. He'd sell you out for pocket change or a quick fix."

"He's my brother."

"And I'm your best girl. You listen to me. I say you go to Mr. Scarpetti right now, tonight, with me, and apologize."

"I can't, Rosie. Anyway, it's all set with Benny. He's picking me up at nine."

"Then I'm going with you."

"No."

"Then you'll die all by yourself."

Charlie walked a few steps away from the protection of the transparent umbrella, away from Rosie, back into the rain. The rain felt colder on his back. When he turned to face her again, he felt shame.

"I used to be good, you know. Really good. I played the Copa once, you know that?"

"Yes, I know."

"Back when I was good, back when I could still take hold, nothing could beat me then. Nothing could move me off my ground. But the jokes, they kept getting thinner, weaker, dumber, and then I needed the booze to do just anything at all up on that stage. If I could just take hold for a while, I could be back at the

Copa again, opening for Sinatra, maybe, or Tony Bennett. I just need some time to take hold. Don't you see?"

"What about those two friends of yours who work for Scarpetti? What if they went and put in a word for you?"

"Johnny Cakes and Jimmy Renzo? Jeez, they'd get in a hell of a mess with Mr. Scarpetti if they tried to help me."

"But they *like* you. They're your best *friends*. You make them *laugh*. And you don't say stupid things about them when you're on stage."

"Okay, but..."

"Maybe they could help."

"Jeez, Rosie..."

"Give them a try, won't you?"

Charlie thought hard for a moment, but then he shook his head. "No, Rosie. I'm in trouble enough. You run along now. Benny, he's due any minute. As soon as I'm safe up there in Connecticut, I'll call you."

"You won't take me with you?"

"I can't."

"All right, then. Run away. I won't mourn you, you know. You already do enough mourning on your own. 'Poor Charlie Thayer. Poor, poor Charlie.'"

"That's cruel, Rose."

"So it's cruel."

"I'll call you. I promise."

"Sure you will."

There was something more she had wanted to say, needed to say, but she kept it from him. Without a goodbye kiss, or even a whispered goodbye, she turned, raised her transparent umbrella over her head, and disappeared around the corner.

Charlie waited another hour in the steady rain. When Benny's old Dodge didn't show, he thought of moving on to another phone booth and trying to reach him again. But when he got to the end of the alley at Pitkin Avenue, Benny's car was at the curb with the motor running. The passenger door swung open, and Charlie got in. Benny half-smiled and squinted from behind the wheel. He was still junkie-thin, but his skin was less sallow, his eyes less sunken, like a starving stray cat that'd just had a full meal.

"What took you?" Charlie asked.

"There was a car. I thought maybe it was following me. It took me a while to shake it. You okay?"

"I'm wet and cold, but you're a hell of a sight to see, Benny. Thanks."

"Not a problem. You ready?"

"Yes."

"Good. You don't need any extra clothes or anything?"

"No."

"You got money?"

"Yes."

"Good. That's good. So, I take you out to the ferry, right?"

"Right."

"I gotta make one stop first. Is that okay? It's over in Red Hook. Then we'll be off."

"Whatever you say, Benny."

"That's good. Won't take long, anyway. This guy I know, he's leavin' town tomorrow, and he owes me a hundred bucks from poker. Gotta get the money from him before he splits. Okay? I'll stake you with some of it."

"Sure. Okay."

"Good. That's good."

The rain let up some on the drive to Red Hook, enough for Benny to turn off the windshield wipers. For the first time in over twenty-four hard, cold, wet hours, Charlie felt his tired body relax.

"You want a smoke?" Benny asked.

"You know I don't smoke," said Charlie.

"Mind if I do?"

"Of course not."

"Good. That's good. You're in a hell of a mess, huh?" He slipped an unfiltered cigarette between his thin lips and handed Charlie a cheap butane lighter. "Light me?" he asked, and Charlie applied the blue flame to Benny's cigarette. "Yeah. One hell of a mess," said Benny, taking a deep draw, exhaling through his nose, and filling the car with smoke.

"I guess so."

"Did you *really* call Scarpetti's wife a fat bitch? Right from the *stage*? And all that other stuff, too?"

"I guess. I don't remember. I was drunk."

"Hell, you're always drunk, Charlie."

"No. Not always."

"Hell of a mess, anyway."

"I'll fix things," said Charlie. "In time. Going to take hold now, Benny. Going to finally take hold. Get back on top. Tenacity. That's what I'm going to have. In spades. Plenty of tenacity. You'll see."

"Good. That's good."

Benny turned the wipers back on when they reached Red Hook. It was after ten and everything was closed.

"Where does this guy live?" Charlie asked.

"Oh, we're not goin' to his place. He's at a gamblin' room down one of these side streets. Damned if I remember which one. Oh, yeah, here it is."

Benny drove down a narrow, cobbled street that seemed to have an outlet at the far end, but when Charlie looked ahead, he saw a high chain link fence blocking the way out. When he turned to his brother, Benny had a .45 automatic pointed at him.

"Get out of the car, Charlie," he said.

"*What?*"

"Get out of the *car*. If you don't, they say I gotta do it myself, with this here piece."

"But, why? *Why?*"

Benny looked like he might cry, but he held back. "I needed a fix real bad, Charlie. I'm sorry. Please, just get out of the car so I don't have to be the one doin' this."

"You're my *brother*, Benny. Why didn't you come to *me* if you needed money, even for a fix. I coulda got it."

"Please, Charlie. Just get out of the car."

"All right," Charlie said, and stepped out into the street. There were no cars parked at the curb, and when Benny's car spun its wheels leaving, there were no cars at all. Only the darkness and the cold and the rain.

Another car turned the corner, a big Pontiac with its lights turned off. It stopped a few feet in front of Charlie, and two men stepped out. Charlie knew the men. They were his best friends. They liked him. He had made them laugh.

"You?" said Charlie. "Scarpetti sent *you* to do it?"

"Sorry, Charlie," said Johnny Cakes in a meek, halting voice. "Mr. Scarpetti, he wants this to be some kind of test for us. Understand? A loyalty test. Believe me, this is the last thing me and Jimmy want to do."

"I'm sorry, Johnny. About what happened at the club. I really mean it."

"We know."

"Will you tell him that for me? Will you tell Mr. Scarpetti that I said I was sorry? Will you tell him that?"

"Sure. We'll tell him."

"I really am sorry."

"So are we."

"Well, then," said Charlie. "I guess this is it, huh?" His impulse was to run toward the chain link fence, but his legs refused to move.

"You can get a head start if you like," said Jimmy Renzo. "We can give you that much of a chance anyway. We might miss, you know. We might miss, shooting into the dark. Or we might just wing you. Maybe Mr. Scarpetti would be satisfied if we just winged you. It's a chance, anyway, Charlie. It's the only chance you've got."

"Do you *want* to run?" asked Johnny Cakes. "Do you *want* to give it a try? Give it a try, Charlie, okay?"

Charlie smiled. He understood now why his legs wouldn't move, why he would stand here, right *here*, as if he'd been rooted to the paving stones. Now, at long last, he was taking hold, getting a grip, standing his ground. He felt good. Blessed, even.

"Remember to tell Mr. Scarpetti that I was sorry," he said after a moment, his voice firm, determined, calm. "I've always been sorry. And when you see Rosie, will you tell her that I...that I didn't...that I wasn't...?"

"Sure, Charlie, sure," said Jimmy Renzo, and Johnny Cakes nodded in sad agreement.

"I really *am* sorry."

"So are we."

Charlie looked down at his feet one more time to admire their steadfastness. Then he looked again at the two men. When they pulled the guns with the silencers from under their raincoats and pointed them at him, Charlie just closed his eyes.

The Hold Up
By Douglas DiNunzio

The old Ford Fairlane was parked outside the Williamsburgh Savings Bank on Hanson Place. It was eight o'clock in the morning, and it was already hot and humid in the Borough of Brooklyn. Two young men sat in the car. Occasionally they glanced at each other, but mostly they stared straight ahead. The sidewalks along Hanson Place were crowded, but there was nobody else just sitting in a car, waiting. The driver, whose name was Carmine, lit a cigarette, and his passenger, whose name was Rico, frowned seriously.

"That'll kill you," said Rico.

"*One* cigarette will kill me?" said Carmine, sneering.

"You know what I mean," said Rico. "It'll kill me, too, if I gotta breathe it with you."

"Your window's open, for Chrissake. Just stick your head out."

"That won't help *you* any."

"So? Whatta you care?"

"Maybe I don't want you to get lung cancer and die, okay? My father, he got lung cancer and died. My Uncle Bill got lung cancer and died. My Aunt Janine got lung cancer and died. And Old Mr. Fazzone down the street, just last month *he* got lung cancer and died."

"And?"

"If I shut my window, and the smoke from your fuckin' cigarette filled the whole fuckin' car, would you stop then?"

"There's *two* windows open in the car, stupid. I can still get fresh air from *my* window."

"*Fresh*? You call that *fresh*? If I can *see* the air -- and I *can* -- then it's not fresh."

"Oh, you can *see* air now, huh?"

"We both know it's dirty. City air is dirty."

"And you can see it, huh? You can see the fuckin' air? You're fulla shit, Rico. You know that?"

"It's a fuckin' figure of speech."

"*You're* a fuckin' figure of speech. That's what *you* are. Jesus!"

"Just sayin'," said Rico.

"You're *always* just sayin'."

As Carmine took a long pull on his cigarette, Rico's left arm swept past him suddenly, brushing the end of the cigarette and spilling ash into Carmine's lap.

"Jesus! What'd you do *that* for?" said Carmine.

"Do what?"

"What you just fuckin' *did.*"

"I was swattin' at somethin'. I'm sorry. Excuse me."

"Swattin'?"

"That's what I said."

"*Swattin'?*"

"Yeah. A fly. I was swattin' a fly."

"Christ Almighty, Rico! What the fuck is wrong with you, anyway?"

Rico's face reddened, and his sallow cheeks puffed. "*What's wrong with me? What's* <u>*wrong*</u> *with me? I got Vincent Fuckin' Price makin' loud buzzin' sounds in my ears, okay, Einstein? I got Vincent Fuckin' Price dive-bombin' me here in this fuckin' car. That's what's* <u>*wrong*</u> *with me, okay?*"

"What?"

"A *fly,* stupid. A fuckin' *fly.* Jesus Christ!"

"Well, watch what you're doin', okay?"

"Sure. Okay."

"Okay, then."

Rico's hard look softened, and then it hardened again. "Don't you ever go to the movies, Carmine? Jesus. *The Fly.* It's a fuckin' horror movie. Vincent Price. He's a fly."

Carmine frowned, and then he smiled. "Oh, yeah? Well, the fly was David Fuckin' Hedison. That's who the fly was. Vincent Fuckin' Price was his fuckin' brother. And anyway, movies are bullshit. Who needs 'em? It's more fun goin' to bed with my Angie. I don't need any fuckin' movies if I got my Angie in the bedroom."

"You're married a whole goddamn six months and you're not tired of pokin' her yet?"

"'Course not."

"Me, it only took two."

"Two times?"

"No. Two *months*, stupid. I still got the wanderin' eye, see, and my Paula, she walks around the flat in a house dress with curlers until past noon."

"Her house dress has *curlers*?" Carmine grinned savagely.

"I'm not even gonna fuckin' *answer* that one," said Rico curtly. "A question that fuckin' stupid doesn't deserve an answer."

"You should talk," said Carmine.

"I'm talkin', yeah."

"You always talk."

They sat for a while in silence.

"My Angie's a natural blonde, you know. She's even got it down there."

"Down *where*?"

"You know..."

"Well, if she's a natural blonde, she would, that's right."

"That's what I fuckin' said."

"And I fuckin' heard you."

"There's only one sure way to tell, you know," said Carmine.

"Yeah. You look at her roots."

"Her *roots*?"

"Her *hair* roots, for Chrissake. If they're brown, she's not a natural blonde."

Carmine frowned. "That's one way, sure, but it's not the best way."

"So, what's the best way?"

"Lookin' down *there*. If you want my opinion, that's the best way, and the *only* way, to tell if a girl really *is* a natural blonde. But you'd have to be on very familiar terms with her, if you know what I'm sayin'."

"Bet *you* didn't find out 'till you were already *married* to her."

43

"Meanin' what?"

"Oh, forget it."

"No, I *won't* forget it. Meanin' what?"

"Never mind. Jesus Christ, Carmine, what a fuck-up you are sometimes."

"Oh, yeah?"

"Fuckin'-A right."

Rico took another unsuccessful swipe at David Fuckin' Hedison and mopped his brow with the sleeve of his shirt. Carmine ignored him.

"Jesus. It's gettin' hot," said Rico.

"*Gettin'* hot?"

"Yeah. So, what's the hold up?"

"*What's the hold up? This. This* is the hold up. Don't you ever listen? You got ears, right? Don't you ever use 'em?"

"We're holdin' up this bank. I *know.* You *told* me already. But I still wanna know *why.* I also wanna know why we're waitin' here in this fuckin' car, in this fuckin' heat. Like, what's the *hold up?*"

"Because the bank's not open, stupid. How you expect to rob a bank if it's not open?"

"Okay. So, explain to me, pretty please, *why* we happen to be sittin' here in the hot sun in your fuckin' car waitin' for the fuckin' bank to open."

"We got here a little early, that's all."

"A *little* early? The bank opens at *ten.* It's fuckin' *eight.*"

"I know it is. We're a little early, that's all."

"And so...?"

"And so we're gonna wait until it opens."

"How we gonna do it?"

"Do *what?*"

"Rob the fuckin' bank, that's what."

"I don't know," Carmine admitted. "I don't exactly have a plan. I guess we just walk in and tell 'em to give us the money."

"Now *there's* a brilliant idea. You got a gun?"

Carmine nearly blushed. "Sort of," he said.

"Sort of? You got a gun or not?"

"I got a water pistol. Hell, it looks like a gun, if you don't look too close."

"Is it loaded?"

"You mean with water?"

"No. With fuckin' *hydrochloric acid*. Jesus Christ, Carmine!"

"I don't wanna hurt anybody. I just need the money. Angie and me, we need the money."

"Couldn't you borrow it?"

"Already tried that. My parents, her parents. Her brother and sisters, my brother and sisters. Her cousins, my cousins, some of the neighbors, the grandparents, even. Maybe I could put in some overtime at the factory, but that would take a while."

"So, maybe you should take a while."

"And maybe I should rob the fuckin' bank."

"The Bickford's across the street is open."

"So, we're robbin' the fuckin' Bickford's now?"

"They got coffee. I could really use some coffee."

"It's fuckin' eighty degrees at eight in the morning, and you want coffee?"

"It's the caffeine. I could use the caffeine. I mean, if we're gonna rob the bank and all..."

"You wimpin' out on me, Rico?"

"'Course not. I just need some coffee."

"Some fuckin' pal you are. Wimpin' out like that."

"I'm not wimpin' out."

"Yeah, you are. Some fuckin' pal. So, what time is it, anyway?"

"Eight o'clock. I just fuckin' told you."

"And the bank opens at ten."

"Like you said, we're early. It won't open for another two hours. So, you wanna rob the Bickford's instead? They wouldn't have as much money, though."

"I don't *wanna* rob anyplace. I kind of *have to* rob the bank, that's all. I thought we covered that fuckin' point."

"You could give up on the pari-mutuels for a while."

"This has nothin' to do with the pari-mutuels."

"So, stop bettin' on the numbers."

"This has nothin' to do with the numbers."

"Can't be poker. You're the luckiest son of a bitch I ever saw at poker. So, what's it got to do with?"

"None of your fuckin' business."

"Oh, I see. I get it now. I'm your best friend since grade school, we were best man at each other's weddin's, and now you want me to help you rob the biggest fuckin' bank in Brooklyn with a water pistol -- *unloaded* -- and all of a sudden it's none of my business why the fuck we're doin' it. That's cute. That's real cute, Carmine. Thanks a lot."

"I made some bad decisions lately, that's all."

"And this isn't one of 'em?"

"Are you gonna stop raggin' on me about this or what?"

"Why you gotta rob the bank, Carmine? Just tell me. Just say it."

Carmine lit another cigarette. He took several long drags and exhaled through his nose.

"Jesus, not again," complained Rico.

"Just lean your fuckin' head out the window."

"That's not what I mean."

"Mind your own business, okay?"

"No! Tell me why."

"Why stick your head out the window? So you won't get my lung cancer."

"You got it *already?*"

"No. I mean, *when* I get it."

"Tell me *why*, damn it. Why we robbin' this bank? Answer the goddamn question."

"Oh, fuck this. Let's go home."

"What?"

"I said, '*Fuck this, let's go home.*'"

"Why?"

"I'll tell you later, okay? It's kind of embarrassing, the whole fuckin' thing. The whole damn business."

"So, somehow it's gonna be less embarrassing if you tell me *later*? And you say *I'm* fucked up?"

Carmine started the engine. Then, just as quickly, he turned it off. For the first time, his eyes showed sadness.

"Hey, Rico, I'm sorry, okay? I apologize."

Rico's eyes were on David Fuckin' Hedison, but his attention shifted just for a moment.

"Sorry about what?"

"You know. All this shit about robbin' the bank. It was a fuckin' dumb idea. I'm sorry I almost dragged you into it."

"Don't worry about it. I already forgot."

"Anyway, thanks for comin' out here with me."

Without looking at Rico, Carmine started to turn the key again.

"Wait. Wait a minute," said Rico with some urgency.

"What?"

"Don't move, okay. Just don't move..."

"Don't move the *car*?"

"Don't fuckin' *move*, okay. Not the car, not you, not your big fuckin' mouth, not anything."

Carmine's lips were forming a scowl when Rico's extended left hand caught him squarely and painfully on the side of his head.

"Christ, Rico! I *told* you I was sorry, didn't I?"

"*Got him!*" shouted Rico. "Got the son of a bitch!"

"Are you fuckin' nuts? Got *who*?"

"David Fuckin' Hedison, that's who!"

"The fuckin' fly?"

"Killed the little bastard dead," said Rico with unbounded pride.

"Oh, that's swell. That's just swell."

"You should be happy, you ungrateful son of a bitch. Flies, they carry diseases."

"Fine. Swell. Anything else you wanna tell me?"

"About?"

"*Flies*, for Chrissake. Fuckin' flies. David Fuckin' Hedison."

"Yeah," said Rico.

"So, what about him?"

Rico offered a grin that had been building up in him for some time. For years, maybe.

"Well, he's kinda all squished up in your hair."

The Absolute
by Douglas DiNunzio

They called him Little Mr. Hurley because he looked so much like the chemistry teacher at the high school. Ever since junior high, Jimmy Tollifer's classmates had teased him about it, and now, as a junior, he found himself in Mr. Hurley's chemistry class on the first day of school, the last period in the day.

Mr. Hurley was a legend at school. He'd gone there himself before being a *summa cum laude* graduate of Harvard University. He was in his forties now, a teacher for twenty-two years. He was not yet married, which was considered unusual because he was so handsome. The girls who weren't terrified of him all had crushes on him. Like most of the boys, Jimmy Tollifer was in awe of him.

"Chemistry, like all the hard sciences, deals in absolutes," he told them on the first day of class. "There is nothing wishy-washy about the hard sciences. No maybes. No sometimes. Water boils at exactly 212 degrees Fahrenheit. It does not boil *sometimes* at 211 degrees or *occasionally* at 209 degrees, but always at 212 degrees. *Always*. If you understand that, even remotely, you might begin to understand the hard sciences. Do *you* understand that, Mr. Tollifer?"

Jimmy had been attentive, and so he couldn't understand why Mr. Hurley had called on him as if he were a slacker. There were others in the room that weren't attentive. Jimmy could hear them whispering in the row behind him. *So, why pick on me? It can't be just because I look like him*, he thought.

"Yes, sir," said Jimmy.

"Yes, sir, *what?*" asked Mr. Hurley, his fierce eyes boring in, his lips forming a small scowl.

"I understand what an absolute is. Sir."

"Let's hope so," said Mr. Hurley, and continued his lecture. He didn't single out Jimmy again, but when the bell rang to end both the class period and the school day, Mr. Hurley looked at Jimmy and said, somewhat threateningly, "I would like to see you after class, young man."

Jimmy watched the others leave the room. Some of them were grinning, others shaking their heads in mock confusion. Soon, they were gone, and Jimmy was alone in the room with Mr. Hurley. He had to wait until Mr. Hurley had finished erasing all the equations from the blackboard before Mr. Hurley finally looked at him.

"So, Tollifer is your last name, is it?" Jimmy had expected a stern teacher's tone, but Mr. Hurley was talking differently now, almost conversationally.

"Yes, sir."

"And your father's first name is John?"

"Yes."

"Tell me a bit about yourself."

"There's not much to tell, sir," said Jimmy.

"Tell me what there is, then."

Jimmy offered the usual information. He was an only child, and he lived with his father, an insurance adjustor. His mother had died two years earlier, of ovarian cancer, and English was his favorite subject. He liked baseball, and he wanted to be a newspaperman when he grew up. Mr. Hurley listened politely, nodding every so often to show that he, too, was paying attention.

"Your mother's name was Sally, wasn't it?" he said after a pause.

"Yes, sir."

"And her maiden name was Russell, was it not? I went to school with a Sally Russell. At this very school, as a matter of fact. Well, then, am I correct? About your mother, I mean."

"Yes, sir," said Jimmy, as politely as possible. "Russell was my mother's maiden name."

"Thank you," said Mr. Hurley. "You are dismissed, Mr. Tollifer."

The next day in class, Mr. Hurley lectured about balancing chemical equations. The students who couldn't demonstrate that ability were kept after class until they could. Jimmy was one of them. And he was still failing at it dismally when the other three students had succeeded and were dismissed.

"I believe you said that English was your favorite subject, Mr. Tollifer," said Mr. Hurley after Jimmy's fifth failure to balance an equation. "Might that not be the reason why you are still here, after all the others have left? English is a poor choice of careers for anyone with a strong mind, and I suspect that you do have one despite your present difficulties with this subject. All the strong minds gravitate toward the sciences. All the virile minds lean in the direction of the great absolutes. Don't you see?"

"Yes, sir," said Jimmy.

"And is chemistry your lest popular subject, then?"

"I guess," said Jimmy.

"Tell me about your mother," said Mr. Hurley suddenly.

"My mother?"

"Yes. What was she like? Was she a good mother to you?"

Jimmy turned away from the blackboard and looked at Mr. Hurley in confusion.

"As I told you the other day, I knew your mother, went to school with her in this very building. You don't have to say anything, of course, if you don't want to. I was just curious, and sad that Sally is no longer with us."

"She was okay, I guess," said Jimmy.

"Only okay?" prompted Mr. Hurley. "Surely more than okay. What were her interests, her hobbies? She must have had hobbies. In our schooldays, she liked to catch butterflies in a net. And at night, fireflies in a jar."

"How would you know that?" asked Jimmy.

"I went out with her, of course," said Mr. Hurley with a smile.

Jimmy turned away from the blackboard and moved a step so that Mr. Hurley could see his work.

"Ah, finally," said Mr. Hurley. "Well done. I'll give you a tougher one tomorrow."

"Tomorrow?"

"Yes. Directly after class. You are dismissed, Mr. Tollifer."

The next day at the end of class, Mr. Hurley wrote another problem on the blackboard. Jimmy stared for a long moment at its complexity, then set out to solve it. He had practiced balancing equations at home the night before. This one was not as difficult as it was time-consuming. He set to work in silence while Mr. Hurley sat at his large oak desk reading a science journal.

"I never knew your father very well," said Mr. Hurley just before Jimmy had finished his balancing act. "He came to town late in your mother's –– and *my* –– senior year. What is he like?" It was more of a diversion than an inquiry, thought Jimmy, as if Mr. Hurley did not want this current session to end too quickly.

"He's okay," said Jimmy. "Like I said, he's an insurance adjustor."

"I see," said Mr. Hurley. "And was he good to your mother?"

"Sure. Especially when she got sick."

"Were they in love?"

It was an odd question, Jimmy thought, but he answered it anyway. "Well, they were *married*," he said.

Mr. Hurley was silent for a moment. When Jimmy stepped aside to show his success on the blackboard, Mr. Hurley said nothing. Jimmy waited to be dismissed, but Mr. Hurley did not dismiss him.

"I have a position open for a student assistant," he said quickly. "Someone to help straighten up the room after school. Perhaps even to correct test papers, help set up the lab. Would you be interested?"

"I guess," said Jimmy.

"Excellent," said Mr. Hurley. "You can start tomorrow. You are dismissed, Jimmy."

For the next three days, Jimmy reported to Mr. Hurley. The work seemed more like make-work than real work, but Jimmy found an unusual pleasure in it, and an even more unusual pleasure in Mr. Hurley's company. At times, Mr. Hurley would ask more personal questions, almost always about his mother, but more often than not they just talked. Mr. Hurley was a Dodger fan, like Jimmy. Pete Reiser, the accident-prone Dodger center fielder, was his all-time favorite. Jimmy's was the colored player, Robinson. Mr. Hurley liked to eat Cracker Jacks at the ballpark, while Jimmy preferred hot dogs smothered in mustard and sweet relish.

"I took your mother to a ball game once," Mr. Hurley said on a Friday afternoon. "A day game at Ebbets Field." It was almost four o'clock, and they had been talking about other things until then. "She was a very popular girl, your mother. It wasn't easy to get a date with her. But she was great fun, you know, and something of a tease. But, then, that's not how you would have known her, is it? The life of the party, that was Sally."

Over the weekend, Jimmy thought he might ask his father about his mother and Mr. Hurley, but his father was busy. He always seemed to be busy. So, on Monday, before school started, Jimmy went to the school library and looked at the yearbooks. His mother and Mr. Hurley were in the class of 1936. His father's name wasn't in the book. The caption under Mr. Hurley's picture read: "Teddy; super serious sometimes; drives in first gear; Harvard bound." The caption for Jimmy's mother read: "Super Sally; great legs and more; flirt much? everybody's girl."

That afternoon, while cleaning up after chemistry class, Jimmy asked Mr. Hurley, "What happened to you after you graduated?"

"The both of us, you mean?"

"Yes."

"Well, I went off to Harvard, and your mother went to...I think it was cosmetology school, but I might be wrong."

"Did you still go out with her after high school?"

"Of course, that first summer anyway. I had to stand in line to get a date with her, but she was a delight, and I was a patient fellow in those days. Very patient, indeed. You had to be if you hoped to get a date with Sally."

"Oh," said Jimmy. "Was she still nice?"

Mr. Hurley offered a serious look. "And why shouldn't she be?"

"Oh," I don't know," said Jimmy absently. He was thinking about the bickering at home, the flashes of temper that he remembered, right up to the day she'd died. He had never known his mother to be happy, and it was comforting to know that she *had* been happy -- really happy -- once.

"It was that first summer before college, I recall, that I carved our initials in the sweetheart tree."

"Sweetheart tree?"

"The one in the park, near the boathouse. The initials on that tree went all the way back to the turn of the century. It was a Dutch elm, if I remember correctly. But it became diseased, and they cut it down. There's only a small plaque there now."

"Oh," said Jimmy. "Well, I'm done with my work. Can I go home now?"

"Of course."

"I'm starting to like chemistry a little more," Jimmy admitted. "I might never be very good at it, not like you, certainly, but it's been better than I thought it would be."

"That's good to know," said Mr. Hurley, smiling warmly. "I'll see you tomorrow. You've got that first big test coming up on Friday. Balancing equations. Think you're up to it? You remember what I said, don't you?"

"Yes, sir. Strong minds tend to go toward the hard sciences."

"And the absolutes. Remember the absolutes."

"Yes, sir."

"Well, good night, Jimmy."

"Good night, Mr. Hurley."

That night, Jimmy had a question for his father. He'd waited until just after dinner to ask, because that was the best time to get his father's attention, just before he started reading the newspaper. Once his father had started reading, there was no interrupting him until morning.

"Mr. Hurley told me that Mother went to cosmetology school after high school. Is that where you met her?"

"And why would I ever expect to meet her there?" he answered coldly.

"I just thought that..."

"I met her on a blind double-date, if you want to know."

"But did she really go to cosmetology school?"

"She did, but she had to drop out."

"Why?"

"She just dropped out, that's all."

"Did you carve her initials on the sweetheart tree?"

"Of course not," he said, and started reading his newspaper. "What nonsense."

Jimmy wasn't quite himself in chemistry class the next day. Mr. Hurley let him clean up for a while, but finally he asked the obvious question. "What's wrong, then, Jimmy?"

"My mother. Do you know why she dropped out of cosmetology school?"

"Who told you that she did?"

"My father."

"Oh, I see."

"Did you know him at school?"

"Not well. He had a terrible crush on your mother, as we all did, but she wasn't keen on him. They met on a blind date, I believe."

"That's what my father told me, yes."

"All the boys she'd been dating, including myself, we'd all gone off to college. If she dropped out, it had to be then. Whatever school she was attending, she was doing quite well in it the last we spoke. Straight A's."

"So, she stopped dating everybody except my father?"

"All the fellows I knew, anyway. As many as there were, the circle that revolved around your mother was still fairly small."

"And then she dated only my father...even though she didn't really like him?"

"Yes."

That afternoon after school, Jimmy went to the park to see where the sweetheart tree had been. The stump was still there, beside the brass plaque. Jimmy tried to picture the various couples carving their initials into it with jackknives, and knowing that his father never would have done that. Why had he married her, then? And why had she stopped dating everybody else? Why marry him if she'd never loved him?

He put the question to his father that night, just before his father picked up the newspaper.

"That's none of your business," he answered curtly. "And it's none of Ted Hurley's business, either."

"You and Mother, you never got along," said Jimmy. "So, why did you marry her?"

"I've told you once."

"You haven't told me anything."

"*Damn Hurley, and damn the rest of them!*" he said, and started to read the paper. Jimmy yanked it away with his hand.

"Damn them for *what?*"

His father was on his feet suddenly, quivering with rage. "And damn you for asking. *Damn you!*" Then he started to cry. Jimmy had only seen his father cry once, talking to Jimmy's grandmother on the telephone.

"I want to know *why*," said Jimmy, matching his father's anger, and ignoring the tears. "Why did you *marry* her? Why did you marry my mother?"

"*So she could have you!*" he shouted. "*So you could be born!*"

"I don't understand," said Jimmy, his own anger fading into confusion.

"*Do you want it spelled out?! Is that what you want?!*"

"No," said Jimmy. He let his father return to the news of the day. He felt an odd pity for his father now. His father's world was empty, devoid of all secrets. Empty and hollow.

The next day at school, Jimmy did not stay after class to help Mr. Hurley clean up. He left with the others, went to his locker, picked up his windbreaker and the books he needed for his homework, and started for home. He was halfway there before he turned back. Mr. Hurley was at his desk, correcting papers. When he looked up at Jimmy, he smiled warmly, as if some grave concern he'd been nurturing had just melted away.

"Ah, there you are! Did you forget? I need you to set up the equipment for the lab tomorrow. Can't do it without you, you know."

"*Are you my father?*" Jimmy asked. His face was frozen in a grimace. It was a look of both anger and pain.

"I don't understand," said Mr. Hurley.

"Then I'll ask you again. Are you my father?"

"Jimmy..."

"*Just look at me! I'm your goddamn reflection in the mirror!* Well, aren't I? That's why the kids call me Little Mr. Hurley, isn't it? They don't understand. They don't know. I didn't understand, either. But I do now. Am I your son? Are you my father? I know all about my mother now. Everything. All about what she was. But I want to hear it from you. You and nobody else. I want to hear the truth."

"You know less about your mother than you think, Jimmy. What a wonderful girl she was...until she met your father."

"He isn't my father," said Jimmy. "He's just the man who married my mother. Or, at least, he was the only one who would, after."

"Jimmy..."

"*Are* you my father? Yes or no? You are, or you aren't. Well, come on, Mr. Hurley. Just say the word. That's your specialty, isn't it -- absolutes?"

Mr. Hurley paused a long time before he answered. And then he equivocated. "There were several of us who could have been your father, Jimmy."

"*Do they all look like you?*"

"Your mother was a free spirit."

"She was a whore. She was a cheap whore who dropped out of cosmetology school. That's what she was. That's *all* that she was. Did you fuck her?"

"I won't answer a question like that, Jimmy. It demeans your mother."

"Are you my father?"

"Jimmy..."

"Are you?"

"I might be."

Jimmy lost no time leaving Mr. Hurley in his classroom. Jimmy's guidance counselor, Mr. Lacey, was still at his desk in the guidance office on the first floor.

"I want out of chemistry class," said Jimmy, storming in. "I don't care what other subject you give me. I just want out."

Mr. Lacey put his spectacles on the desk and looked up. "Well, you'll need another math or science class to graduate. You're not doing well in chemistry?"

"I'm doing fine."

"Then why do you want to drop the class?"

"Personal reasons," said Jimmy.

"Well," said Mr. Lacey, "there's trigonometry, and there's calculus. But you nearly failed algebra and geometry. Are you absolutely sure that you want to switch?"

Jimmy thought for a long moment, and then he smiled. It was only after he'd smiled that he could give his answer.

"Yes," he said. "Absolutely."

A Shooting on Plymouth Street
by Douglas DiNunzio

Johnny Boy and Tommy were in the Bickford's on Fulton Street in late afternoon. It was cold outside and overcast, but it hadn't started snowing yet. Johnny Boy was staring with sullen eyes at his coffee and cherry pie as Tommy read the current edition of the *Brooklyn Eagle*. Occasionally, they glanced out the window at Fulton Street. Finally, Johnny Boy looked up from his coffee.

"Okay," he said. "I say we hit that Yid Nasserman's pawnshop. He's got gold, jewelry, and cash in there."

"Mr. Nasserman ain't no Yid," said Tommy. "You shouldn't talk about him like that."

"Well, he talks Yiddish, don't he?"

"He ain't no Yid. And he ain't no Kike, neither. He's just Jewish, that's all. He's a nice man. And we ain't gonna rob his shop. Not unless we wanna get plugged. Ever since he got robbed and beat up a couple months back, he's got himself a .45 that he keeps under the counter. And we can't try it at night, either, 'cause he's taken to livin' upstairs."

"Okay, so who *are* we gonna hit?"

Tommy leaned across the table and lowered his voice to its most conspiratorial level. "There's a factory down on Plymouth Street, near the Navy Yard. Consolidated Furniture. Strictly wholesale, strictly cash-and-carry. There's a moneybox in the office on the third floor. The armored car doesn't come around until Friday morning –– that's tomorrow –– so there might be a couple grand in there right now, maybe more."

"And how do you know all this?" asked Johnny Boy with a small sneer.

"This guy I know, he worked there. Cased the place for weeks. It's a lead pipe cinch, he says. There might be a night watchman, but they're never armed."

"So, this guy you know, why isn't *he* doing the job?"

"He's been screwin' a mobster's wife. Had to leave town in a hurry. Said he'd tell me about it only if he was cut in for ten per cent of the take."

"That's kind of steep, and him not even bein' here."

"Well, those were his conditions, and I gave him my word."

Johnny Boy scowled. His dull eyes brightened. He brushed back his cowlick. "You're some kind of Boy Scout, you know that?"

"I gave him my word," said Tommy, returning the look. "And we're gonna rob the factory, like I said." At twenty-one, Tommy was the older of the two, and he expected to be in charge.

"Okay, if we're going to do the job, let's go," said Johnny Boy, and stood up.

"It's too early."

"It's dark right now," Johnny Boy complained.

"Not dark enough. Not quiet enough over there, either. Best if we wait until about ten o'clock."

"And what do we do until then?"

"Catch a movie," said Tommy.

The movie was over at eight, and Johnny Boy and Tommy drove around for a while in Tommy's car.

"So, how's Ted? How's your big brother doing these days?" asked Tommy.

"Okay, I guess."

"Heard he lost his job at the Navy Yard."

"They're cuttin' back. Got almost as many ships mothballed as ones in service. It's okay, though. He's been lookin' for another job. Goes to the employment office every day. Why, I don't know. It'll be chump change, whatever he gets."

"And we're better than that, huh?" said Tommy, showing some sarcasm.

"Yeah. A *lot* better."

"Okay, okay. No need to get sore about it."

"Listen up, Tommy. I ain't gonna be no ass-kissin' stooge like my brother. Not ever. Understand? I'm gonna *be* somethin' in this world."

"Sure, sure," said Tommy. "He livin' at home now?"

"Until he gets back on his feet, yeah. Mom gave him back his old bedroom."

"He's an okay guy, your brother. You could learn a thing or two from him."

"Yeah, yeah. Change the subject, okay?"

"Sure," said Tommy. "Have it your way."

They drove around. Past the Soldiers' and Sailors' Arch in Grand Army Plaza, past Ebbets Field, heading roughly west toward the Navy Yard and the warehouses. There was a Salvation Army band playing in front of their headquarters on Quincy Street.

"Pull over," said Johnny Boy. "I wanna listen."

It was a small contingent, four uniformed men with trumpets, and two young women with hymnals. The women were singing to a small, shivering crowd.

What a fellowship, what a joy divine,
Leaning on the everlasting arms:
What a blessedness, what a peace is mine,
Leaning on the everlasting arms...

"That's pretty," said Johnny Boy. "Maybe I shoulda tried to be a preacher or somethin'. I like the music, anyways."

"We don't have to do this, you know."

"Yeah," said Johnny Boy. "I know."

"So, we still doin' it?"

Johnny Boy looked at his watch. "It's time," he said.

"We don't have to do it."

Johnny Boy bristled. "Well, if we *don't* gotta do it, then we're gonna do the pawnshop. I ain't scared of that Yid Nasserman. Not when I got this." He opened his coat. There was a .32 caliber revolver in the waistband of his trousers.

Tommy turned off the motor. For a moment, he wished he was alone in the car.

"Where'd you get the piece?" he asked finally.

"Whatta you care?"

"That's trouble," said Tommy. "That's real trouble."

"Relax. The gun can't be traced," said Johnny Boy. "So, what's it gonna be? The Yid or the factory?"

"I don't like it when you talk like that," said Tommy. "You don't even sound human."

"What's it gonna be?"

Tommy started the engine, and they pulled away from the curb. Johnny Boy folded the flap of his coat over the revolver. He was listening to the Salvation Army music again.

Leaning, leaning,
Safe and secure from all alarms;
Leaning, leaning,
Leaning on the everlasting arms...

"Sure is pretty," said Johnny Boy, and patted his revolver.

It was dead quiet on Plymouth Street when they arrived just after ten. Looking up, they saw the great undercarriage of the Manhattan Bridge. One of the towers of the Brooklyn Bridge filled the view at the end of the street. The faint glow of the streetlights danced in little star shapes on the surface of the East River. A light snow was falling. Tommy pulled the car to the curb but kept the engine running.

"It's this one right here," he explained. "There's a loading dock around the corner. That's where we break in. We'll park around the next corner, on Jay Street. Okay?"

"And where's the moneybox again?"

"Third floor office. I'm tellin' you. Piece o' cake."

"Yeah, sure," said Johnny Boy, and Tommy drove past the dock, turned the next corner, and parked. Johnny Boy already had the revolver in his hand.

"I told you that was trouble," said Tommy with a baleful look. "You won't need it here. There's no reason to bring it inside."

Johnny Boy smiled a rebuke. "I'll keep it anyway. Just in case."

"Have it your way," said Tommy.

"I plan to," said Johnny Boy.

"All right, now listen. I got a crowbar in the trunk. That's how we get past the loading dock door. I got a flashlight, too. The stairs are on the left. The office is halfway down the hall, third floor, on the right."

"Or so says your pal."

"You got a problem with this job?" asked Tommy.

Johnny Boy rested his hand on the handle of the revolver. "Yeah, I just might," he said, smiling again.

"Okay. I'll say it once more," said Tommy. "If you don't like the setup here, we can just go home and call it a night. If it don't look right to you, I mean. Don't matter to me."

"We wouldn't be goin' home in any case," said Johnny Boy, his sly smile more like a smirk now. "We'd be goin' go to that pawnshop and havin' it out with the Yid."

"What the hell is wrong with you?"

"Nothin'. I'd just like to shoot it out with the Yid, that's all. It'd be some fun."

"What you got against him, anyway? What you got against Mr. Nasserman?"

"He's a Yid, ain't he?"

Tommy started to raise his hand at Johnny Boy, but then stopped and took a moment to calm himself. Johnny Boy took notice of the threat by widening his smile and patting the handle of his revolver. Tommy opened the driver's door, stepped out, walked to the back of the car, and opened the trunk. When he came around to the passenger side, he had the crowbar and the flashlight in the same hand. He opened the passenger door and glared at Johnny Boy with barely suppressed anger. "Listen up," he said, almost snarling. "We're doin' this place -- and *only* this place -- and then we ain't never doin' nothin' again ever, you and me. You and me are quits after tonight. You got that? *Quits.*"

"Sure, sure," said Johnny Boy, grinning back fiercely. "Never knew you had such a soft spot for Yids."

The loading dock door gave way easily, quietly, almost without sound. Tommy glanced inside before cautiously pushing the door open. He moved the beam of his flashlight around the great, dark hollowed-out space that greeted him. Johnny Boy came in after him, and the revolver was in his hand.

"Pretty big place," observed Johnny Boy, flashing another grin.

"Bigger than both of us," said Tommy, without smiling. And suddenly Johnny Boy was ahead of him, taking the stairs two at a time. When they reached the third floor landing, Johnny Boy stopped to wait for him. Tommy moved the beam of the flashlight down the long, narrow hallway ahead of them.

"The company office is on the right," Tommy reminded him. "Halfway down. And take it easy. You go stompin' around, and the watchman's gonna hear you."

"It's a big place. Plenty big. And who says they even got a watchman here, anyway?"

"Just take it slow and easy. That's all I'm sayin'. Don't take chances him hearin' you."

"Got this if he does," said Johnny Boy, waving the revolver.

The office door was unlocked. Tommy opened it and moved the beam of the flashlight around. There were several large desks in the room. The moneybox had to be in one of them. A moneybox with at least two grand in it. Tommy completed the arc and started to scan the room again when he stopped in mid arc. He gasped. Johnny Boy saw it, too.

A safe.

"*What the hell?*" shouted Johnny Boy.

"It looks new," said Tommy. "They musta just installed it."

"*So, what the hell do we do now?*" Johnny Boy shouted again.

"We get outa here," said Tommy.

They heard the sound from the end of the corridor the moment they entered it. A flashlight beam washed over them.

"*Hey!*" shouted a voice, and then, "*Jesus!*"

Johnny Boy was immobilized only for a moment. The beam of light was fully on his face, blinding him, when he fired twice. The flashlight at the end of the corridor hit the hard floor, the bulb shattering. The watchman fell, too, but neither Johnny Boy nor Tommy heard him. The loud report of the gun was still echoing in their ears when they reached the door to the loading dock. Another light was suddenly on them, from the street. Johnny Boy fired a shot at the light, and two soundless bullets sought him out. One hit the door of the loading dock, and the other struck him in the side.

"*Jesus! I'm hit!*" he shouted, and Tommy grabbed his arm, pulling him toward their car around the corner from the alley. "*Son of a bitch shot me!*"

"*A cop shot you!*" Tommy shouted back. "*What the hell did you shoot the watchman for?*"

Tommy pushed Johnny Boy onto the passenger seat, slammed the door, stumbled to the driver's side and started the engine. The driver's door was still open as he pulled away, turned at the first corner on Jay Street, sped down Sands Street, and then Flushing Avenue, finally heading eastward. Johnny Boy was holding his side and groaning.

"Jesus, I'm bleedin'. I'm bleedin' bad."

"Kings County Hospital's about twenty minutes away," said Tommy. "I'll get you there."

"No. No hospital. Jesus, Tommy, I'm dyin' here. I gotta talk to a priest."

Johnny Boy raised his left hand. It was bloody.

"You're not dyin'. You're just shot."

"I'm dyin', I tell you. Can't you go any faster?"

"Cops'll stop us."

"I'm goddamn dyin' here! I need a priest!"

65

"We've gotta get rid of the gun," said Tommy.

"Jesus, I'm bleedin' t' death!"

"Hospital first," said Tommy.

"No. Take me home! I wanna go home!"

"Okay, but we gotta get rid of the gun."

"The gun? The gun? I'm dyin' and you're worried about the gun?"

Johnny Boy rolled down the window and threw the gun into the street. *"Okay? Satisfied?"*

"Jesus!" said Tommy.

"Get me home, and then send for the priest!"

"Okay, okay. Jesus! You threw the gun out the goddamn window? Jesus Christ!"

Johnny Boy's mother lived on Kingston Avenue in Crown Heights, over a market. It was a main street, but not busy at this hour. Tommy pulled the car to the curb.

"You go in first," said Johnny Boy. "Make sure the coast is clear. Then I'll come in. Tell my mom to call Doc Mitchell." After some thought and a brief examination of the wound, Johnny Boy had agreed that he didn't need a priest.

"You sure you wanna do it this way?" asked Tommy. "Brooklyn Jewish Hospital's real close."

"It's a goddamn Yid hospital," complained Johnny Boy. "I ain't goin' t' no Yid hospital. Just tell my mom I'm out here. I'll be up in a minute."

But Johnny Boy was still in the car when his mother came down from their third floor apartment, awash in tears.

"It's okay, Ma," he said, and they went inside.

"What happened?" she asked when Johnny Boy closed the door of the apartment behind them and slumped into a chair in the parlor.

"Some guy tried to rob us near Borough Hall. He had a gun. I got shot." Johnny Boy looked to Tommy for confirmation, but Tommy just stared at him.

"Why didn't you go to the hospital?" asked his mother, the tears still flowing. "Why'd you come here?"

"You know what the doctors do when they see a bullet in somebody? They call the cops. Think anybody would believe me, with my record? Just call Doc Mitchell. He won't tell anybody."

"Mind if I leave now?" said Tommy.

"Stick around," said Johnny Boy. "Hey, Mom, where's Ted? Where's my straight-arrow big brother?"

"He's working tonight," she said. "The employment office called right after you left. He's working someplace right now."

"Where?"

"He didn't say. A night shift someplace. Oh, he was so happy to be working again. I've been waiting up for him."

"When's he due back? I gotta talk to him."

"Well, he gets off around midnight, or so he told me."

Johnny Boy looked at his watch. There was dried blood on the face, and he scraped it off to read the hands. "It's almost one now," he said.

"He has to take the subway home. Is it still snowing?"

"Yeah, kind of."

"I'm calling the doctor now," she said, and disappeared into a bedroom. Tommy made a move toward the door.

"Where you going?" said Johnny Boy with some alarm.

"I told you. We're quits, you and me. On account o' you, I'm a goddamn accessory to homicide, or attempted homicide if that watchman's still breathin'. You're crazy wild, Johnny Boy, and you're rotten mean on the inside. I don't like you any more. We ain't friends any more."

"Aw, come on, Tommy. Hey, I was just kiddin' about wantin' to plug old Mr. Nasserman."

"No, you weren't. And if I ever hear you talk that way again, I'll beat the crap out of you."

"Sure, sure, Tommy. Hey, come on. Stick around. You gotta help me explain things to Ted."

When Doc Mitchell arrived, Johnny Boy was in a cold sweat. He was in his bedroom now, stripped to his underwear.

"You're one lucky son of a bitch," Doc Mitchell said. "Bullet went right through. It's just a flesh wound, but I'm going to have to clean it out. That's going to hurt." Doc Mitchell glanced up at Johnny Boy's mother. "Do you have a clean washcloth? We need to stuff it in his mouth while I put this swab in the wound. He'll probably pass out from the pain, but if he doesn't, I don't want him biting his tongue off."

"Where the hell's Ted?" asked Johnny Boy. "I need him here. I need him now. Right now. Things always turned out okay when Ted was around."

"I don't know," said his mother. "Maybe his subway train got stalled."

"I want Ted," said Johnny Boy, at the edge of tears. "I want my brother."

"We'll tell you as soon as he's home," said his mother.

"Time to put this swab in," said Doc Mitchell. "I'm going to give him a shot of penicillin after that, just in case, and then I'm gone. And remember, please, if the police come. I wasn't here tonight. You haven't seen me."

"They won't come," said Johnny Boy, his bravado resurfacing for a moment. "Nobody knows what happened. Nobody saw us. Not enough for an identification, anyway."

"You said you were shot in a *hold up*," said Johnny Boy's mother.

"Aw, Mom," said Johnny Boy. Doc Mitchell pushed the washcloth into his mouth, and then the swab roughly into the wound, and Johnny Boy passed out.

Johnny Boy awoke only for a moment after Doc Mitchell had left, then fell asleep on his bed. Johnny Boy's mother closed the door to his room, and she and Tommy went back to the parlor. Tommy sat on the couch as Johnny Boy's mother stood quietly at the window overlooking Kingston Avenue. It was still snowing, but the snow was heavier now. To Johnny Boy's mother, the snow cover looked almost like a shroud.

"I'm real sorry," said Tommy. "It's partly my fault, what's happened."

"He was never much like Teddy, you know," she said. "Always looking for the easy way, always thinking the world owed him a living."

"Maybe this'll turn him around," said Tommy.

"And where is Teddy, anyway? Where is that son of mine? He should have been back hours ago."

"Ted'll be here. And Ted'll straighten him out. Honest."

"I hope so. Would you like some coffee?"

"No, thanks."

"Only take a minute."

"No, thanks. I really should be going. My folks are gonna wonder where I am."

"Look. There's a police car down there," Johnny Boy's mother said suddenly, but without alarm. "It's pulling up to the curb."

"Is the dome light flashing?"

"No," she said. "What does that mean?"

Tommy walked to the window and looked down at the police car. "It means they're not in a hurry," he said stiffly. "It means they're not coming for Johnny Boy."

"Oh, thank God," she said.

"Yeah. Thank God."

"Why else would they come here?" she asked. When Tommy didn't answer, she asked again.

"To see someone else in the building, I guess."

"For what reason? If they're not...in a hurry?"

"They have to make condolence calls sometimes," he said, and turned away from the window.

"Condolence calls?"

"That's what I've heard."

"Goodness," she said. "Everyone else in the building is probably asleep."

"They'll wake them," said Tommy. "If they have to."

"Oh, I wish Teddy was here. Why is he so late?"

"I don't know," said Tommy, his heart pounding in his chest, his stomach churning. "Honest to God, I don't know."

"I hope Teddy did well his first night on the job. Are you sure I can't get you some coffee?"

"Well, okay, I guess," said Tommy, and he felt his mouth go dry.

She called to him again from the kitchen. "Black, or with cream and sugar?"

"Black," he said, his throat constricting. "Black as night."

He was at the door now, listening to the heavy footfalls on the stairway. He had hoped –- prayed -- to hear them stop at one of the two floors below, to hear someone else's door opening; but they hadn't stopped. Then, with an uncommon suddenness, they were on the third floor landing. All at once, Tommy's legs seemed to give out from under him, and his lungs burned in his chest. There was a light tap on the door.

"You want a doughnut with that?" Johnny Boy's mother asked from the kitchen.

"Sure," said Tommy, and began to cry.

The Ice Cream Man Cometh
by Douglas DiNunzio

The 18th Avenue Gang had settled into their clubhouse in Larry Chandler's basement that Saturday morning, waiting for Hickey. But now it was mid-afternoon, Hickey still hadn't arrived, and the members were getting anxious.

"So, where's Hickey?" asked Jack.

"How should I know?" said Billy.

"Don't worry," said Larry, sitting by the refrigerator that his parents kept down there. "He'll come."

"Well, he'd *better* come," said Rocky, absently combing his hair. "He's always the life of the party. And hey, he always comes for Larry's birthday."

"Don't worry. He'll be here," said Larry.

"Sure will be great to see him again," said Wally.

"He's not gonna start lecturin' us again, is he?" asked Eugene. "Last year, that's all he did. I got damn tired of it."

"He just wants us to better ourselves, that's all," said Billy. "Just like he did for himself. I mean, he don't smoke or drink no more, and he's got a job, even. Salesman, I heard."

"He *had* a job. A *year* ago. Doesn't mean he's still got one," argued Eugene. "Doesn't mean he gave up smokin' and drinkin', either. Just means he doesn't do any of that stuff when he comes back home to Brooklyn every year. Don't mean a thing."

"Damn straight," added Jack. "That Hickey's always had a big mouth. And he's a con man, always has been. Can't believe a word he says."

"What's with you guys?" said Larry. "Hickey, he's always been good to us. Real good. He's a pal. He's the life of the party."

"Well, I don't wanna hear any of that hokey stuff when gets here and starts preachin' again."

"About?"

"About us and what he keeps callin' our pipe dreams. Accordin' to Hickey, we're tryin' to live our pipe dreams and goin' nowhere. Like we got to break out of here and stop livin' like losers. Losers, huh? Well, as I recall, Hickey quit school in the seventh grade. He always acts like he's doin' better than we are – that he *is* better -- but I don't believe a word of it. And he never gets around to provin' anything anyway."

"He always dresses nice, though. A three-piece suit last time. Brooks Brothers. Successful guy, that Hickey."

"That don't mean anything. He coulda pinched it."

"Well," said Rocky. "Maybe he's not so right about us, but maybe he's not be so wrong, either. I mean, what do we *do* every Saturday but come down here and waste the day away with small talk and booze?"

"What's so bad about doin' nothin'?" argued Jack.

"Nothin', long as you're doin' somethin' the rest of the time. What're *we* doin'? Nothin', that's what."

"I think Hickey's honest-to-God worried about the bunch of us," said Larry. "Yeah, that's what I think. So let's cut out the grousin' and give the guy a nice big cheer when he comes down those cellar steps."

"He won't get no big cheer out of me," said Eugene.

"Aw, come on."

"No, I mean it."

"What's your gripe about him anyway?" asked Billy. "He never did anything bad to you."

"Okay, here's what I'm talkin' about. You remember that kid used to come down here and hang out with us? Hickey used to call him Mr. Tomorrow. Remember him?"

"Sort of."

"Well, I heard just yesterday. He's up at Bellevue in the nutcase ward. Got the DT's. Twenty-three years old, and he's a full-time drunk. And Hickey, he convinced the poor slob that all he had to do was shake off his devils, stop believin' in his pipe dreams, and he'd be happy. And is he happy? No. He's in Bellevue."

"But maybe he's happy there," said Wally.

"What?"

"Who says a guy can't be in Bellevue and also be happy? Maybe he's finally at peace with himself."

"Jesus. Now you're soundin' like Hickey."

"And what's wrong with that?" said Larry. "You remember how, last year, Hickey said we should all settle down and get married? Well, *he's* married, and it didn't seem to do him any harm."

"He *told us* he was married. He ever show you a wedding ring, or a marriage license, or a picture of his bride? 'Course not. I tell you, he's a con man. He's been connin' us since junior high."

Larry laughed. "You remember that story Hickey told us about how his mother must've had a turn in the hay with the ice cream man, on account of Hickey didn't look anything like the guy he said was supposed to be his father? In the hay with the ice cream man. Ha ha!"

"I thought it was the milkman," said Wally.

"Nah. The ice cream man," Larry insisted. "That's who it was. Pretty funny guy, that Hickey. Some of you can grouse about him, but I can't wait to see the old goofball again. Even if it's just for a day. Hickey, he's an ice cream man, too, kind of."

"Yeah," said Jack, scowling. "You can always count on Hickey to screw somebody else's wife."

"I don't mean it that way," said Larry. "I mean, he always brings somethin' good when he gets here."

"You just like him because it's *your* damn birthday he comes back home to celebrate," said Eugene. "We got birthdays, too, you know. I might like him better if he treated us the same."

"Sure he does."

"That's bull. Hickey, he's like a bad dream, a ghost that won't let the livin' alone."

Larry stood up quickly. "And who says we're livin', Eugene?"

"I do, that's who. Me, I like the way things are. Today is just fine, and tomorrow...well, tomorrow can damn well take care of itself. I don't need to be preached to. If I wanna hear a sermon, I'll go to church."

Wally frowned as he took a pull on his beer. "I want to do like Hickey says, but I got too much bad luck. Lookin' for work, even. I mean, bad luck just follows me around. There's no shakin' it off, either."

"So, you come here and have a good time with your pals. What's wrong with that?" said Eugene.

"Well, nothin', of course. But..."

"So shut up and drink your beer, Wally. Stop bein' a drag."

"Hey, lighten up, everybody," said Larry. "Jesus!"

"What?"

"Just lighten up, okay? Hey, Wally, light me."

"Oh, light yourself. I'm goin' out for a breath of air."

"Jesus, why's everybody gettin' so sore?" said Larry. "Hickey's comin', for cryin' out loud. All the way from Ohio. We're gonna have some fun once he gets here. Some real fun. Come on back, Wally."

But Wally had already walked up the basement steps and was gone.

"Come on, everybody," said Larry. "Let's stop grousin' about Hickey and all."

"Well, I got a question," said Eugene. "I heard a story about a month ago. Guy told me Hickey got arrested for beatin' up his wife. Guy who knew Hickey from back in Ohio."

"*What* guy?"

"Just a guy. Over at Nero's."

"And how would *he* know?"

"He just told me, that's all."

"That's bullshit. Hickey loves his wife. Says she's the one who turned him around in life. You remember last year when he told us? Stopped him drinkin' and smokin', made a new man out of him. He's just crazy about her."

"Well, that's what the guy told me, anyway. And here's my point. We all know Hickey's a con artist. He's a salesman, right? To be a salesman, you *gotta* be a con artist. Well, maybe Hickey's learned to con himself, too. Not just us. Not just his customers, but himself, too. Maybe you gotta do that first if you're gonna con other people. Maybe you gotta con yourself first."

"And what's he conned himself into?"

"Believin' his own lies, maybe. Like maybe his wife is really a nag and he hates her guts, but he wants to believe he loves her, so he does the big con on himself. You con yourself, believe me, you can con anybody and everybody."

"I don't believe that for a minute," said Larry.

"That's because you don't want to. Nobody likes to look like a jerk."

"Hey, Jack, get me another beer," said Larry, ignoring the taunt.

"Think about what I'm sayin'," said Eugene. "Hickey, maybe he means well. But if he's conned himself, how's he ever gonna know what the truth is? What if he's lyin' to himself every time he opens his big mouth?"

"So, ask him yourself when he gets here."

"*If* he gets here."

"And where'd Wally go?"

"Out for some air."

"Now, Wally, there's another one," said Rocky. "He always says he's got bad luck, and that's why he can't get a job. That's why he hangs out down here with us, drinkin' and smokin' his life away. Well, I happen to know he coulda got a job drivin' a Yellow cab couple of months ago. He turned it down. Bad luck? That's bullshit. Maybe he's gone and conned himself, just like Hickey. Just another excuse to make up so he can blame somethin' or somebody else for his troubles."

"Troubles?" said Eugene. "Who's got troubles? What's wrong with what we got here? We're havin' fun down here, and that's a fact. Trouble? I don't have any trouble."

"You don't have a job, either."

"A job don't necessarily make you happy. Money don't make you happy, either."

"A job can get you a future, though. Twenty years from now, where are we all gonna be, huh? Down here in Larry's parents' basement, smokin' and drinkin' and talkin' trash? I don't think so. But we're gonna be someplace or other, and that's a fact. And if we're lucky, or unlucky, we're still gonna be alive. But that's it? That's all we're gonna be? Just alive?"

"So? What else do we have to be?"

"Jesus, we gotta have some kind of purpose, don't we?"

"I don't know," said Rocky. "I just don't know."

"You all sound like Hickey," said Eugene, offering a sneer of contempt. "Just exactly like Hickey. You've all gone and conned yourselves, that's what you've done. So, we gotta have a purpose now, huh? Chains. That's what you get when you got a purpose. And freedom is what you lose."

"Chains?"

"By 'purpose' I'm guessin' you mean work, right? Well, to me, work is chains."

"You really think so?"

"Yeah, I really *think* so. And tomorrow will damn well take care of itself."

Wally appeared suddenly at the top of the basement stairs. He was out of breath.

"I saw him!" he shouted. "I saw Hickey, just on the next corner!"

"So, is he comin'?"

"I guess."

"You *guess*?"

"Well, he was talkin' with a couple of cops on the corner in front of the deli. You should see him! Three-piece suit, and smoking this big cigar. Lookin' like the president of General Motors. I suppose he'll be along shortly. Hot damn! He's finally here!"

"Well, let the good times roll!" said Larry. "Beers all around, for when Hickey gets here."

"Hickey's hangin' around with cops now?" asked Eugene.

"He was just talkin' to 'em. He'll be along shortly."

"Him and his high talk about pipe dreams, ha!" snorted Eugene. "Tomorrow will take care of itself. Mark my words. And don't mark nothin' Hickey says about nothin'. The big blowhard. Now he's even buddies with the cops. And he's *smokin'*, too."

"Didn't you hear what Wally said? He said he was *talkin'* to them. Outside the deli. Just talkin'."

"Where are those beers?"

"They're comin'."

"Hey, Wally, go on back out there and speed him up," said Larry. "Tell Hickey we're waitin' for him so the party can get started. Hell, we got enough beer in the frig to go on an all-day bender. Life of the party, that's Hickey."

Wally bounded up the steps and was gone. For a few moments, the basement room became quiet.

"I had a job offer couple of weeks ago," said Jack in a timid voice. "Part-time school custodian over at the high school. My dad knows somebody in the Board of Education."

"And?"

"Been thinkin' about it."

"And how long you gonna do that?"

"I don't know. Just thinkin', that's all."

"Well," said Eugene, "when Hickey does get here, I'm gonna get the straight dope if I gotta beat it out of him. I mean it. I'm sick and tired of his bullshit. *Don't smoke, steady job, loves his wife* -- that's all bullshit."

"Hickey's okay in my book," said Larry. "Say what you want, he's okay by me."

"He's as phony as a three dollar bill."

"Oh, is he? Listen, Eugene. Hickey's the only successful guy in this whole bunch. What's so bad about havin' a little success and convincin' other guys to maybe have some, too? If he *was* a liar or a phony, he wouldn't be wearin' a Brooks Brothers suit. Well, would he? And the way he talks about his wife and all. You can't fake that. I know he adores her, and you guys oughta know it, too. Hickey, maybe he's right about the pipe dreams. I mean, sure it's fun just hangin' around down here, but maybe Hickey's the only one of us who's got things figured out. Maybe he's worth another listen. Just maybe, okay?"

"You ever meet his wife?" said Eugene. "Well, I never have."

"Yeah, we know. And you never saw a weddin' ring, and you never saw a marriage license, like he's going to carry one around with him."

"He didn't have a ring, and that's a fact."

"So why didn't you call him on it back then?" asked Rocky. "Why make us have to listen to you a whole damn year later. You're the one that's conned, Eugene. Hickey doesn't think like you do, so you don't like him. I say you're jealous. That's why you're flappin' your gums about him all the time."

"Hey, come on, you guys," said Larry. "This is supposed to be a party, and Hickey, he's supposed to be the guest of honor. Come on, now."

"Well, where is he? And where's Wally? He get lost on the way to the deli or something?"

"I'm here," said Wally, standing at the top of the basement steps. He descended slowly, as if he were walking through a minefield. Hickey wasn't with him.

"So, where's Hickey?" asked Larry, trying to read the odd expression on Wally's face.

"He's not comin'."

"Not comin'? Why?"

"Cops got him."

"The ones on the corner? The ones you said he was just talkin' to?"

"Jeez. I can't believe the cops were after Hickey."

"They weren't," said Wally. "He turned himself in. That's what one of the cops told me, anyway, while the other cop was puttin' the cuffs on him."

"Why would Hickey turn himself in?" asked Larry. "It's not like him. I mean, back in the days when we were all in trouble, Hickey, he was an ace at talkin' himself *out* of trouble. And now he turns himself in? For what?"

"Killin' his wife. Put a bullet in her head when she was asleep. Told the cops he did it because he loved her too much, that he wasn't good enough for her."

"That's a con if ever I heard one," said Eugene. "You don't kill somebody you're crazy in love with. Which means Hickey didn't love her. Which means he lied to us about her all along. All part of the con job he's been workin' on us for years."

"Jesus. He killed his wife? Where? When?"

"Columbus, Ohio, sometime yesterday. He shot her in the head, got on the first train headed here, stopped the first cops he found, and turned himself in."

"Jesus."

"I just can't believe it."

"Not Hickey."

"I'm takin' bets the son of a bitch pleads insanity," said Eugene, sporting a grin for the first time. "He'll talk himself out of the hot seat. Con everybody in the damn courtroom. So, who wants some action? I'm givin' three-to-one odds."

"Oh, shut up, Eugene."

"Jesus," said Wally. "I don't feel so good."

"Hickey, he was our rock."

"And it was all a lie, what he was tellin' us?"

"Looks that way."

"No, I just can't believe it. I *won't* believe it."

"I hope that part-time job's still open," said Jack.

"Put away the beer," said Larry. "I'll have my mom brew us up some coffee."

"The party's over."

"I guess."

"Hard to believe."

"Jesus. Not Hickey."

"And all this time, too."

"He fooled us good, huh?"

"Time to grow up, maybe. Time to get serious."

"You really think so?"

"Bullshit," said Eugene. "Live for now and let tomorrow take care of itself."

"Shut up, Eugene. Just shut up."

"Jesus. No more Hickey. Whatta we do now?"

Girl on a Pedestal
by Douglas DiNunzio

Morton had met her on a blind date arranged by his sister. Her name was Elise, and she was pretty but not beautiful. Her skin was smooth, but it was also pale, as if she seldom ventured outside. Her blouses were long and puffy, more little girlish than stylish, and her skirts tended toward plaids. She wore conservative shoes. She was maybe twenty or twenty-one years old-- he'd never asked her age. He adored her, but she did not feel the same about him. Much of the time when they were out somewhere together, he thought she was merely tolerating him until someone better came along. She could be moody, she could be rigid, and she was easily disappointed in people.

Their first date had been a movie -- Abbott and Costello -- but he couldn't remember the title, and they didn't talk about it afterward. Conversation with Elise could be difficult, even painfully so. It was hard to find a subject that interested her. When she did speak, it was usually to argue about something he'd said innocently enough. She had opinions about almost everything, and most of them were negative. On their second date, another movie, she took offense when his eyes glanced casually at her blouse. He would argue that he was only admiring the pattern, but she'd seen it as an attempt to judge the size of her breasts.

"That's rude, you know," she said. "Ogling. Is that all that boys can think about? Imagining what their dates look like without any clothes?"

"I was only admiring the pattern," he said half-heartedly. "Where did you get it? It's nice."

"Bloomingdale's," she answered. "It was on sale. And you were ogling."

"Well, it's a nice blouse, anyway."

He really *had* been imagining the size of her breasts. At times, he even tried to lag a step or two behind her to catch the gentle sway of her hips. Wasn't that the purpose of a date, anyway, to size up the woman who might be the future mother of your children? And didn't girls size up boys the same way? Isn't that why some boys stuffed socks down the fronts of their pants? But he didn't dare try to talk about things like that with her. She was always on her guard, always too prudish, and too defensive, to permit it. This was going to be a difficult romance, a walking-on-eggshells romance, if it was ever going to be a romance at all.

Their first dinner date was yet another setback. He'd taken her to a nice restaurant in Manhattan, a place with atmosphere, real waiters, tablecloths and a full list of wines.

"That's the wrong fork," she said when he started on his salad. "And your water glass is to the right of your plate, not the left, just above your knife."

"I think President Eisenhower's doing a pretty good job, don't you?" he said, putting his fork down awkwardly. He hadn't tried discussing politics with her before, but all the other avenues of conversation became dead ends so quickly. Politics was only a last resort before complete silence.

"Are you a Republican, then?" she asked.

"No, not really, but I think he's doing a pretty good job."

"If you're not a Republican, then why do you think he's doing a good job?"

"I don't know," he said. "I just think he is."

"You don't know very much about politics, do you?" she said, and another topic of conversation was put to rest.

That night, by the time he'd escorted her to the door of her apartment in East Flatbush, he had finally worked up the courage to kiss her goodnight. She let him, but there was no ardor in the way she returned the kiss.

"I had a swell time tonight, Elise. Did you?"

"It was okay."

"Is it all right if I come in for a few minutes? Just to sit and talk? It's still early, and..."

"I don't think so," she said. "My roommate has to get up at five. She's a stewardess."

"Oh? What airline?"

"Pan American."

"Oh. That's swell. Bet she travels a lot."

"That's what stewardesses do," she said.

"I promise not to stay late," he said.

"I don't think so." Her hand was on the doorknob.

"I never *have* asked you," said Morton, trying his best to stall, to hold off the inevitable. "Where do you work?"

"In Manhattan."

"Oh. Are you a schoolteacher? You look like you might be a schoolteacher."

"No, I'm not a schoolteacher."

"Oh. What *do* you do?"

"Nothing that's any business of yours. It's only part-time, anyway. I'm putting myself through college. I might become a schoolteacher some day, but that's not an immediate goal."

"Oh."

"And I really must say goodbye, you know."

"Well, good night, then."

"No, Morton. I said I really must say *goodbye*. Not good *night. Goodbye.*"

"Goodbye?"

"That is correct." She opened the door and took a step inside.

"Look, Elise, I'm sorry about dinner. I don't know much about fancy place settings and all. Can't you give me another chance? I really like you a lot, and..."

The door closed in his face.

A week later, Morton was at the Eagle Tavern on Canal Street having a beer with his best friend, Solly. He was still grieving over the loss of Elise, and still blaming himself for the failure to win her. Solly was supposed to console him, but it wasn't working.

"She sounds like a real *prima donna* if you ask me," said Solly, "and a prude, to boot. What the hell you wanna hang around with a stiff dame like that for?"

"I don't know. I just liked her. I mean, she could be nice at times, just not often, that's all. You remember that book you told me about -- *The Winning of Barbara Worth*? Well, that's how I felt about her. If I could just impress her a little, she might come around and start to like me."

"Did you try to make out with her?"

"Heck, no. She isn't that kind of girl, and she let me know it right away. I can tell you for sure, Solly."

"You didn't even cop a feel?"

"For cryin' out loud, Solly! What've I just been tellin' you? I was just hopin' she'd come around about me, that's all."

"Well, it sure looks like she didn't," Solly said, frowning. "Maybe you *should've* tried to cop a feel. Maybe that's what she wanted all along. Maybe she was just waitin' for you to try."

"Believe me, Solly, that's the last thing she wanted. She expected me to be a gentleman or somethin', but I just didn't measure up. I'm still crazy about her, really I am, but it looks kind of hopeless now. I keep thinkin' maybe I'll call her and ask her out again, but she'd just hang up on me."

"You put her up on a pedestal, that's what you did," observed Solly grimly. "Worst thing you can do with a girl. Especially the ones that already got their noses in the air."

"You think so, Solly? You really think so?"

"Of course. You put her outa reach. You gave her some slack when you shoulda been reelin' her in. Most dames, they *say* they want the kid glove treatment, but what they really want is for you to squeeze their tits in the darkest part of the picture house or to slip a hand up their skirt. Sure, they make a fuss when you try it, but that's what they really want. You shouldn't be puttin' girls up on pedestals, and that's a fact. Especially that kind. Take it from me."

"This is all kind of depressing," said Morton.

"There's a cure for that," said Solly. "It's called Uptown."

It was only the middle of the day when they went uptown, and most of the bars were quiet. No girls anywhere. Not the kind like Elise, anyway. The more Morton thought about her, the more depressed he became. Maybe he just wasn't good enough for her. Maybe that was it.

"Wanna go to a strip show?" asked Solly after the third bar they tried hadn't panned out. "They got one o' those live strip shows a couple of blocks from here."

"I don't know. They're kind of cheesy, aren't they?"

"You want *real* girls, you go to a strip show," said Solly.

"I guess."

Solly stopped a few doors down, at a storefront. The sign read: PEEP LAND. "Hey, this is even better than a strip club. You go in, you stand in this little room, you put coins in a slot, a panel opens, and you see a naked girl going around and around on this pedestal thing. And she's got nothin' on. Absolutely nothin'. When the panel closes after a minute or so, you put in more money so you can keep lookin'. I think it's maybe four quarters for a minute. There's a guy inside gives you the change. You wanna go in?"

The man who gave out change was a small hunchback named Zoltan. He stood before a tall, cylindrical metal structure with individual doors that led to about twenty-five coffin-sized booths. Each booth had a coin slot and a speakeasy-sized slot for viewing. The structure was at the back end of the store. The front part was magazines, dirty movies, and French postcards.

"You put your money in -- four quarters -- and you get one minute," Zoltan explained. "You want a second look, it's four more quarters. How many quarters you want?"

"I'll take five dollars' worth," said Solly.

"The same," said Morton, and they found two unoccupied booths. Morton stepped inside his and closed the door behind him. There was a small locking mechanism like the kind in public toilets. At first, the stench in the booth was so strong that he almost unlocked the door and walked out. But finally, he put in his quarters.

As he waited for all four coins to drop and the viewing slot to open, he thought about what Solly had said. The girl inside here was a real girl, the kind of girl a guy should go for. No head in the clouds, no affectations. None of that stuff. A real honest-to-gosh woman.

The slot opened, he saw her, and the sight froze him. She was naked, all right. No G-string, no pasties. He could see everything. And she didn't even have to move to display her wares. She was on a rotating stage, a moving pedestal of sorts. The pedestal turned so slowly that the viewing slot closed before he could see her behind. He put in four more quarters for another minute of viewing time, and this time she was just coming around again. Her body was smooth and whitish-pale, but then, he decided, that might be because of the lighting, which was harsh. Morton put in another set of quarters, and another after that, and another, until he'd used up his five dollars. He left the coffin-sized booth, freed finally from the rancid smell, and walked outside. Solly was waiting for him at the bus stop a few feet from the entrance.

"Hot stuff, huh?" said Solly. "See what I mean? That's a real woman in there. That's the real deal. So, where you wanna go next?"

Morton smiled as if to hide his embarrassment. "I think I'll stick around a while. Maybe catch her when she comes out."

"Aha," said Solly. "Got the hots for her, huh?"

"Sure do," said Morton.

"I had one hell of a woody in there," said Solly.

"Me, too," said Morton, lying.

"So, you're really gonna try and get a date with her?"

"Why not? She's my kind of girl, like you said. Everybody's kind of girl."

"Tell me all about it tomorrow, will you?"

"Sure."

"See you tomorrow, then, you horny bastard," said Solly, and hopped on the bus.

She didn't come outside for another hour. There was only one exit, through the storefront, and Morton was content to wait for her there. He wondered how she'd be dressed this time -- in a fancy, stylish outfit, or in conservative clothes: puffy blouses, plaid skirts, flats. He guessed conservative, and he was right.

"Hello again," he said, when she recognized him.

"Hello," she said. "Been waiting long?"

"Not really."

"That's good. So, did you get a good look in there?"

He smiled. It was an unusual smile for him, because there was some pluck in it. "I donated a whole five dollars toward your college education," he said.

"How nice of you. Any disappointments, surprises?"

"Your breasts are bigger than I thought they'd be. And your behind is maybe a little smaller, but I liked them anyway."

"So I was right. You *were* trying to undress me with your eyes."

"Not all the time. It's like I told you. I liked you. I still do, just a little differently now."

"In there," she said, gesturing. "Did you touch yourself while you were looking at me?"

"No."

"I can't ever see who's watching me, but I can hear the grunts sometimes. At the end of the day, they have to hose the whole place down."

"I guess."

"When I first started, I used to wonder who was looking at me so discreetly through those little windows. It bothered me, too. Zoltan told me it was mostly businessmen. Guys in suits. That was kind of a surprise, because I'd expected construction workers, steamfitters, stevedores, bums even. Now, of course, I don't care who's looking. It's just a job. And I'm good at it. Do you know, when I'm in there, all twenty-five of those little window slots are open. I can hear the coins dropping, and then dropping again. That's how good I am."

"Are you busy tonight?" Morton asked with a suddenness that surprised him.

"Now, wait a minute. We're not jumping to conclusions here, are we?"

"I hope not. "

"If you're getting any ideas, if you're at all wondering, I *don't* take my work home with me. Do you understand that?"

"Sure I do. I *do*, really. I just like you, that's all. I promise not to talk about anything you don't want to talk about. And I know what fork to use for the salad now. I studied up on it. Whatta you say, Elise?"

"Well, I'm hungry enough. You build up an appetite under those hot lights, and that's for sure."

"I can take you to dinner, then?"

She smiled. It was a smile she'd never shown him before, and it was a smile he knew somehow that he would see again soon. "Only if you act like a gentleman," she said.

So, This Nun Walks Into A Bar
by Douglas DiNunzio

So, this nun walks into a bar on Empire Boulevard a little after midnight. Not the Audrey Hepburn kind of nun, but the kind that looks like a penguin. Outside, the rain that's been fallin' like cold, sharp needles all day long has just stopped. The bartender, whose name is Joe or Hank or Gus, he asks the nun what she wants, and she says, bold as brass, "Two Irish whiskies." The bartender says, "*Two?*" She says, "I'm waitin' for somebody," and he says, "So are we all, Sister. So are we all." And he happens to notice while he's pourin' her drinks, 'cause she's sittin' right there in the bright light, that she's got a scar runnin' from the point of her chin to one of her earlobes, or at least as close as you can come to where her ears are covered by that tent she wears on her head, and he says to himself, "Tough convent." Then this priest comes in, and he don't look like a regular priest, either. His clerical collar, it's on crooked, he looks like he's covered with pixie dust or somethin', and he's got a wild shock o' red hair that reminds Joe or Hank or Gus of Harpo Marx. And so he says, again just to himself, because it would be kinda unsociable to say it out loud, "Jesus, the circus must be in town." Anyway, the bartender figures that this priest is the one the nun's waitin' for, but then the priest goes and sits at the other end of the bar and orders a scotch and soda. "How's it goin'?" the bartender asks him while he's pourin' it, and the priest says, "Sorry, but I'm not at liberty to say." Well, as you could guess, the place gets real silent after that. The bartender, he goes back to washin' glasses, which is what he was doin' when the penguin nun walked in. Hell, he figures, it's none o' my business what they're doin' here, as long as they pay for their drinks. And if they get rowdy or indecent, I can just call a cop. Then he thinks what a wacky idea that would be, havin' to call the cops on a nun and a priest cuttin' up in a bar past midnight, and *his* bar at that. Not the kind of thing you see every day, and a hell of a story to tell the grandkids once you've had a bunch o' grandkids. But the two of them, they're just sittin' there by themselves and not botherin' anybody. Not that there's anybody to bother, since there's just the nun, the priest, and the bartender in the entire place. Well, about now the bartender gets tired of washin' glasses, and he gets to wonderin' who's gonna come into the place next. Got to be somebody. The nun, she's still got that extra glass of Irish whiskey in front of her, like she's savin' it for a friend, and she's not even lookin' at the priest, so that means that somebody else is gonna walk through that door pretty soon. Who's it gonna be, anyway? The Archbishop o' Canterbury? Lou Gehrig? Little Orphan Annie? But still nothin' happens. Finally, the bartender, he walks over to the nun and he says, nice as can be, "Can I freshen that for you?" even though he knows that she's been savin' it for somebody and hasn't had a drop of it herself. Come to think of it, she hasn't touched the other glass, either. At first, she doesn't even look up at him, but then she does, shows him that long scar again, makes a sour face, and shakes her head like she wants him to go far away and not come back. The bartender, he can tell she's peeved at him for standin' there askin' dumb questions, but then he goes over to the priest and asks him the same thing. "Sorry, I'm not at liberty to say," says the priest, which is what he said the last time, too. So, now, the bartender starts lookin' at the clock over the front door. I mean, seriously lookin'. It's a good hour before he's gotta close, and he's got this feelin' now like the walls are closin' in on him. He's got the penguin nun with the scar at one end of the bar, and the goofy lookin' priest covered with pixie dust at the other, and nothin's happenin', which is worse -- a lot worse, believe me -- than if the nun was doin' a slow strip tease on her stool or if the priest was swallowin' swords down at his end. It was gettin' really creepy-crazy in there, if you know what I'm sayin'. I mean, Alice in Wonderland could be walkin' in there next, with that smilin' cat on her shoulder. To keep himself from goin' nuts while all this is goin' on, the bartender starts washin' glasses again. He's even washin' *clean* glasses now. Anything to keep his mind off his two loony customers. That lasts all of a minute or two, because the priest suddenly picks up his shot glass and waves it in the air like he wants more of the same. The bartender, he goes over, and he's ready to pour the scotch ahead of the soda, but then the pixie dust priest shakes his head, puts his hand over the top of the glass, which is still full, and asks, "How far is it from here to Duluth?" As he says it, he looks down the bar at the nun and gives her a wink. The bartender, somehow he doesn't get the question, so he asks, "In highway miles?" And the priest says, "Or as the crow flies. Either way." Now, the bartender, he's got a *Rand McNally World Atlas* in his little office room in back, and he says to the priest, "Well, I could have a look at the atlas. I'll just be a minute," and the priest says, "Go right ahead and look. I'm in no hurry." And as the bartender turns, he can see the penguin nun with the scar, and she's lookin' right past him at the goofy priest and grinnin' like one of those cats that crazy Alice carries around on her shoulder. The bartender, he goes back to his little office back there, and he's tryin' to find the atlas. It's a pretty big book, but there's all kinds of other stuff piled on top of it. Finally, he finds it, dusts it off, since it's been ten years or more since he's needed to look at it, and he goes back into the bar. But the bar, it's empty. The penguin nun and the crazy priest, they're both gone, and they've taken their shot glasses with 'em. Well, the bartender, he's miffed now. He's upset. They haven't paid for their three drinks, and now they've taken his shot glasses, too. Without thinkin', he looks up at the clock over the door. It's just after midnight, and the rain that's been fallin' like cold, sharp needles all day long has just stopped. The front door opens, and this nun walks into the bar. Not the Audrey Hepburn kind of nun, but the kind that looks like a penguin.

Flying Down to Rio
by Douglas DiNunzio

Afonso Almeida worked at Klein's Hardware on 86th Street. He was forty-six years old. He had no family to speak of outside of Lisbon, and what family he did have there was best not spoken of. He had worked at the store for almost fifteen years now. It was a livelihood, but it was also hard, repetitive, demeaning work. The owner, Mr. Klein, was not an evil man, but he had no compassion, no soul. He could be as hard as his merchandise.

For the first two years that Afonso had worked there, mostly in the stock room, Mr. Klein had insisted on calling him Alfonso.

"I'm not Italian, Mr. Klein," Afonso would say, and so from that time to the present, Mr. Klein just called him Al.

Afonso's personal habits were as tightly regulated as his time at the hardware store, if not more so. He did not like to call it a routine, but it could not have been anything else. Breakfast at 7:00, always cereal with black coffee; lunch at the Woolworth's counter down the street on 18th Avenue, always a hot dog and a Coke; dinner in front of the television with a frozen meal from Swanson and a nice glass of inexpensive port wine. After dinner, if there was nothing interesting on television, Afonso went to the movies. The Benson Theater at 19th Avenue and 86th Street was the closest, but he was willing to travel farther, by foot, city bus, or the BMT Line, if the feature appealed to him.

Afonso never saw the same film twice. To do so would have compromised his routine, which had been well practiced since coming to work at the hardware store, and which was almost an emotional necessity now. He liked "B" Westerns mostly. Johnny Mack Brown, Gene Autry, Roy Rogers, Tim Holt. The movies were one of the best ways to make him forget the hardware store and Mr. Klein. Sometimes he liked other kinds of films -- the Charlie Chan whodunits, the comedies, the costume dramas -- but he had no interest in musicals and would never knowingly spend his money on one.

The past week had been especially hard at work. Mr. Klein was seventy-five and going senile. The more he forgot what he was supposed to be doing at the store, and the more Afonso had to remind him of such things, the more angry and abusive Mr. Klein became. The best time of the day, outside of the lunch hour and just going home at five o'clock, was when Afonso had to make a deposit at the bank on 20th Avenue. It wasn't a long trip, and it was only once a week, on Friday, but it was a sweet respite from Mr. Klein and a chance to see what was playing at the Benson. The current feature was *Dead Man's Gold*, a Lash LaRue Western, so Afonso made plans to see it right after dinner on Friday night.

But dealing with Mr. Klein came first.

"Al, get me some boheles of turprentine from the stock room," said Mr. Kline. Mr. Klein could not pronounce the words 'bottles' or 'turpentine', but Afonso knew what he meant.

"How many bottles, Mr. Klein?" Afonso asked.

"Many?"

"Yes, sir. How many?"

"How many what?"

"Bottles of turpentine, sir, and what size?"

"Who said I wanted turprentine?"

"You did, sir."

"Well, *get it*, then."

The movie was as expected: Lash LaRue and his sidekick Fuzzy brought a gang of claim jumpers to justice. What was unexpected was the coming attraction, *Flying Down to Rio*, with Fred Astaire and Dolores Del Rio. It was an old film, from back in the Thirties. It was also a musical, which, under normal circumstances, Afonso would have dismissed out of hand. But it was set in Rio de Janeiro, in Brazil. They spoke Portuguese there. Not in the film, of course. Afonso was convinced that no one in the picture could actually speak Portuguese. Unless it was Hollywood's sad version of Portuguese.

"*Que piada,*" said Afonso under his breath. "*Quao falso. Quao estupido.*"

When he went home that night after Lash LaRue, he had a thought he had never had before in all of his forty-six years: if Mr. Klein would give him some well-deserved time off, maybe he could go somewhere exotic. Somewhere like Rio de Janeiro, where they spoke real Portuguese. There he could learn to dance the samba and the carimbo. There he might meet the girl of his dreams. *Que adoravel!* he thought. *Quao estimulante!* He could certainly use a vacation. Anything that would get him away from Mr. Klein for a while. He even had his passport from his last sad visit to Portugal, when he had attended his mother's funeral.

But Mr. Klein was not the only impediment to Afonso's dreams of happiness. There was also the widow lady, Mrs. DiRienzo, who lived in Apartment 3C, just down the hall. She was three or four years older, singularly unattractive, and completely without shame. The crude -- and sometimes lewd -- notes she slipped under his door were offensive enough, but even they were not nearly as bad as personal contact in the hall. Afonso would do anything not to meet her there.

"Ah, Mr. Almeida," she chimed in a loud, singsong voice when she met him precisely there that evening after Lash LaRue. "Been to the pictures again?"

"Yes, Mrs. DiRienzo."

"They've got a musical in next week. Musicals are so romantic. Would you take me?"

"No, Mrs. DiRienzo."

"Oh?"

"No, I won't take you, and please stop asking. And please stop putting those *bruto*, those *repugnante* notes under my door. Do your children know you use words like those?"

"It's called *Flying Down to Rio*," said Mrs. DiRienzo, as if she hadn't heard him. "The movie, I mean. You'll enjoy it. We can eat popcorn, do a little necking, yes?"

"Such language," said Afonso. "Shame on you. Your children..."

"I've told you time and again, Mr. Almeida. I have no children."

"Well, go away, Mrs. DiRienzo. Please, just go away."

"You say no, but I know you really mean yes," she said, grinning wickedly at him through brownish teeth. "I can be very romantic, you know, especially in the dark."

"*Que bruxa*," he said aloud after he had slammed his door in her face. "*Que prostituta.*" And the rest of the evening was ruined.

Saturday mornings were always better, if he could avoid Mrs. DiRienzo in the hall. Saturday mornings he went to visit the little girl, Emily, in Apartment 2D. Afonso was like a member of the family there, and he was always welcome. When Emily's parents went out for an adult evening occasionally, Afonso kept the little girl company. Emily was six years old, and she loved Afonso dearly. She would even give up her morning television shows to have pretend tea with him. But this time, it was Emily's mother, not Emily, who answered his familiar tap-tap on the door.

"She's watching television," said Emily's mother.

"I will come back, then," he answered with a little sadness. His visits with Emily were the only tonics, the only real joys, in his life.

"Oh, she still wants to see you, but she can't leave the television right now."

"Can't?"

"She's watching *Winky Dink*. She only got the kit in the mail yesterday."

"*Winky Dink?*"

"She'll explain," said Emily's mother.

Emily was sitting only inches from the television set when Afonso approached. She appeared to be drawing something on the television screen with a black crayon. She had not seen or heard Afonso's approach.

"Isn't she a little close to the television?" he asked her mother. "And why is she writing on the screen?"

"I'll let her explain," said Emily's mother, and left him there.

"Emily?" he said.

"Oh, hello, Mr. Almeida," she said brightly.

"What are you doing?"

95

She smiled at him, and then she turned quickly back to the screen. "Winky Dink is in terrible trouble. He's trapped inside a room, and I have to draw a door for him so he can get away. See?" She finished drawing the doorway, and the little cartoon character walked through it.

"Oh," said Afonso.

"He looks kind of like Speedy Alka-Seltzer, doesn't he?" said Emily. "He really does." Afonso was familiar with the commercial, so he said yes, but still he did not understand.

"Speedy has a tummy tablet for a body, and Winky Dink doesn't, but they look a lot alike, don't you think?"

"Why are you drawing on the television?" asked Afonso. "Isn't that bad for the television?"

"I'm drawing on my Magic Window," she said. "It came with my Winky Dink kit. See? It goes right over the television screen. I also got four Magic Crayons, and even an erasing cloth. Now, when the show comes on, I can help Winky Dink whenever he gets into trouble. It's fun. It's magic."

"Magic?" said Afonso.

"Just think, Mr. Almeida! What if you could draw a door on the television and then walk through it, like Winky Dink. Walk into a whole new world somewhere. Wouldn't that be wonderful?"

"That would be nice," said Afonso. "That would be very nice, Emily. Do you think I could get one of these kits, too?"

"They're not sold in stores," she said, "but you can send for your own kit, if you like. It's only fifty cents, and I've got the address.

"Well, I'll have to think about it," said Afonso.

Mr. Klein was worse than usual on Monday morning. He was having trouble with his eyes, and he kept rubbing them. The more he rubbed his eyes, the worse his mood became.

"Why aren't you doing something?" asked Mr. Klein.

"I opened up and marked all the new stock, and I swept out front. Is there something you want me to do?"

"Something! Anything!" said Mr. Klein, scowling and rubbing his eyes. *"Don't just stand there!"*

"Can I get you some eye drops from the pharmacy?"

"What?"

"Eye drops."

"I don't need eye drops! There's nothing wrong with my eyes! Mind your own business! And do something, for God's sake!"

It was not until Wednesday that Afonso asked Mr. Klein if he could get time off. He didn't have enough money in his savings to fly to Rio, but maybe a week at Coney Island or the picture shows on 42nd Street in Manhattan would be within his budget.

"I need you here," said Mr. Klein sourly.

"It would only be for a week or so," Afonso explained. "I have some time coming."

"I told you. I need you here," said Mr. Klein, and walked away, back to his office. He had a bottle there, and Afonso was hoping past hope that he would not open it. He was always worse when he opened that bottle.

Mrs. DiRienzo was in the hall again that night.

"I've ordered a pizza for us," she said. "Come to my apartment and we'll eat it."

"No, thank you, Mrs. DiRienzo," said Afonso.

"Aren't you hungry?" she asked, and winked at him.

"Of course, but..."

"Then come right in. You know you want to."

"I would rather have lung cancer and die, Mrs. DiRienzo," he said. "I would rather be hit by a speeding train or eaten by crocodiles. I would rather have rabies. Do you understand?" Then he ducked into his room. Suddenly, he felt ill. He skipped his Swanson dinner, skipped television, and went to bed early.

By Friday, Mr. Klein was in the foulest mood that Afonso had ever seen. He complained about everything. He even spoke rudely to his customers. Afonso smelled liquor on his breath, which meant that the day would only get worse. And so it was the purest joy when Mr. Klein handed him the money pouch and told him to deposit it at the bank. *Flying Down to Rio* had been playing at the Benson for a week. Afonso still had no interest in seeing it, but for a reason he could not entirely understand, one of the 8x10 stills in the display case outside the box office caught his attention and held it: a dozen or so beautiful women, standing on the wing of a biplane flying past Sugarloaf Mountain. Suddenly, he found himself looking inside the money pouch. In the next moment, he was counting out the bills. He had never done that before. Not in all his fifteen years working at the hardware store. He had always carried the pouch to the bank, handed it to the teller, turned his eyes away discretely while the teller counted the money inside it, and then taken the deposit slip back to Mr. Klein. There was a great deal of money in the pouch. More than he had imagined. He closed the pouch, and his eager eyes returned to the 8x10 image of the women standing on the wing of the biplane. He did not continue on to the bank, nor did he return to the hardware store. Instead, he just went home in the middle of the day.

Mr. Klein was too drunk on Friday to miss Afonso or the bank receipt until late Saturday, and his lapses of memory kept him from calling the police until Monday afternoon. When a police detective knocked on Afonso's door an hour later, Afonso did not answer, so the detective went looking for the building superintendent, Mr. Marsh. On his way to the super's apartment, he met young Emily on the second floor landing.

"Are you looking for Mr. Almeida?" she asked.

"Why, yes, I am," he said. "How did you know I was looking for him?"

"Just because," said Emily. "Anyway, if you're looking for Mr. Almeida, he's gone away to someplace called Rio Januario."

"Oh?" said the detective. "How do you know that?"

"He told me."

"When was that?"

"The same day he got his Winky Dink kit in the mail. He'd been waiting for it all week."

"Winky Dink kit?"

"Uh huh. He's going to Rio Januario that way."

"What way?" asked the detective, as Emily's mother appeared in the doorway of their apartment.

"What are you telling this man, Emily?" she asked. There was a look of puzzlement in her eyes.

"Just that Mr. Almeida has gone to Rio Januario with Winky Dink."

"Ma'am?" said the detective, looking at her.

"Oh, Emily, really," her mother said. And then to the detective, "It's foolishness. She's just a child."

"Do *you* know where he is, Ma'am?" asked the detective. "I'm with the police."

"Oh, my," said Emily's mother, and gasped. "Has Mr. Almeida done something wrong?"

"We hope not, but he's missing from work at the hardware store on 86th Street, and so is some money he was supposed to deposit at the bank at noon last Friday."

Emily's mother was poised to defend Mr. Almeida, but then she saw Mrs. DiRienzo standing on the second floor landing, her arms full of grocery bags. "Well, hello there," said Mrs. DiRienzo. "Lovely day, isn't it?"

"This man is looking for Mr. Almeida," said Emily's mother. "Have you seen him?"

"He was supposed to take me to the movies Friday night. That nice musical down at the Benson."

"And you haven't seen him?" asked the detective.

"No. He's gone missing. He would never pass up a date with me, so I suspect foul play. Mobsters, maybe. Or a homicidal maniac. There are plenty of those around." She continued up the stairs to her apartment.

"Oh, dear," said Emily's mother.

"He didn't answer my knocks on his door," said the detective. "When was the last time you saw him?"

"Well, we always see him Saturday mornings. He comes to spend time with my daughter. But he didn't come on Saturday. It was strange, him not coming."

"But I *told* you, Mother," said Emily. "Mr. Almeida's gone away with Winky Dink. He *told* me he was going. He said he couldn't stay here anymore. I wanted to go with him, but..."

"Oh, Emily, *really*."

"Well, that's what he *said*."

The detective's demeanor changed suddenly, along with the tone of his voice. "Ma'am, would you send the child away for a moment?"

"Please...?"

"Just send her inside for a moment."

But Emily was already on her way, closing the door behind her. When she was gone, the detective gave her mother an official look. "Did Mr. Almeida seem troubled lately? Depressed? Anxious?"

"No. Not especially. Why?"

"As I said, Mr Almeida might have stolen some money from his employer. Sometimes, an amateur thief gets depressed about what he's done. He gets an attack of conscience and...well..."

"Oh, I see."

"You didn't happen to hear any strange noises coming from his apartment, did you? Of course, I'll ask the other tenants as well, but..."

"Noises? I don't understand."

"Muffled noises, like a gunshot, perhaps. You'd only have heard one if..."

"No," she said. "No, I heard nothing. Nothing at all. Oh, God. Do you think he...?"

Before he could answer, Mr. Marsh, the building superintendent appeared. "May I help you?" he asked.

"I'm looking for the building super."

"You've found him," said Mr. Marsh.

"I'll need the key to Apartment 3B, the one rented to a Mr. Afonso Almeida," said the detective, showing Mr. Marsh his badge.

"Is there some trouble?"

"I hope not."

Emily's mother did not follow them up to the third floor. She went into her apartment, where Emily was waiting for her, smiling broadly.

"I hope Mr. Almeida is having a lot of fun in Rio Januario," she said.

"That's Rio *de Janeiro*," her mother said.

"No, it isn't," said Emily.

Mr. Marsh took the detective to the door of Afonso's apartment. He was about to open it when the detective stopped him.

"Does your tenant own a handgun?" he asked.

"Mr. Almeida? Oh, I hardly think so," said Mr. Marsh, smiling nervously.

"Well, just in case," said the detective, and produced his service pistol from the holster under his suit jacket. "Better stand back," he said, and took the key from Mr. Marsh.

He opened the door slowly "Mr. Almeida?" he asked, but there was no answer. After a cautious moment, he stepped inside, Mr. Marsh trailing behind. The room was empty. The television was turned off, and the small screen was blank. On the floor beside the television were four crayons, a piece of white cloth, and some thin paper packaging. Beside them, on a chair, was an empty money pouch. A thin, clear piece of plastic had been stretched across the television screen, and someone had drawn a small doorway on it with black crayon. Over the doorway was printed a single word: *liberdade*! The detective stared at the screen in puzzlement for a moment, then turned to Mr. Marsh.

"Do you know what that means?" he asked, but Mr. Marsh didn't know, either.

Anthony
by Douglas DiNunzio

"Get me a beer, Anthony," growled Joe Rodino. "Make it a Ballantine, and make it quick."

"Sh...Sure, Joe."

"Well, don't just stand there!"

Anthony shuffled clumsily over to the cooler. It was Friday night, poker night, and it was hot in the room. The room was two floors up a wooden staircase in an old warehouse in Red Hook, a hideout of sorts for Big Dom Spicciati and his crowd. Joe Rodino was Big Dom's underboss.

"It's hot as hell in here," said Joe Rodino. He took off his jacket and draped it over the back of his varnished wooden chair. There was a red leather shoulder holster under his left arm with a .38 revolver in it. "Turn on the goddamn fan, Anthony, and bring me the goddamn beer."

Anthony froze in place. There had been too many commands all at once, and the look on his face told Joe Rodino and the two other men that he didn't know which chore to perform first.

"You *heard* him, Anthony, for Chrissake," said one of the other men. His name was Victor. "Get the goddamn beer. Get us *three* goddamn beers."

Anthony hobbled back to the poker table. His left arm hung limply at his side, and he dragged his right foot like Boris Karloff. A bicycle wreck at age seven -- one of Big Dom's cruel little jokes when he was only a punk hoodlum -- had left Anthony's left arm without feeling. Several operations on his legs had made it possible for him to walk again, but it was an awkward, shuffling gait at best. Anthony was only half a man physically, and there were many in Joe Rodino's rough crowd who considered him just this side of feeble-minded as well. Anthony's handicaps cut no slack with the hard men who worked for Joe Rodino.

"Deal the goddamn cards," said Joe Rodino. The dealer, a small, wiry man named Gaetano, had been shuffling while Anthony went to get the beer from the cooler. Their game of five-card draw was only an hour old, but already Joe Rodino had lost too much money. He glowered at his cards and then at the other two men at the table. Then his cold eyes settled on Anthony. Anthony handed the men their beers with a white-gloved right hand. He was going back to turn the fan on when he stopped suddenly and gave Joe Rodino an unfamiliar look.

"Is there some goddamn reason why you're lookin' at me like that?" asked Joe Rodino.

Anthony didn't answer.

"You're a moron, Anthony. You know that? An idiot. And what's the glove for? You been wearin' that glove -- *one* stupid glove -- all the time for the last couple weeks. What the hell for?"

"I don't know, M...Mr. Rodino," said Anthony. "I...I just like to wear it. It f...feels good."

"Nobody wears *one* glove, *capisce*? And a *white* glove, yet! You look like a faggot."

"He *is* a faggot," announced Victor with a smirk. Victor was large in all the places that Anthony was small, but he was still a nobody. Everybody in the room was a nobody except for Joe Rodino. Big Dom Spicciati and Joe Rodino were men you did not disrespect. They were somebodys.

The three men laughed at the familiar insult, and Anthony's lower lip trembled slightly. "It's noisy in here," said Anthony with a half-grimace, turning on the fan and sending a hot breeze through the hot room. "There's too many voices."

Joe Rodino laid his cards down. He grinned savagely. "Too many voices, huh? What the *hell* is wrong with you, Anthony?"

"He's just goofy," observed Victor. "A goofy cripple, that's what he is."

Anthony looked at Victor and smiled his idiot's smile for a longer duration than usual. A thin stream of clear drool dripped down his chin. He didn't wipe it away. "Everybody's too noisy," he said.

There was a knock at the door.

"Who the hell is that?" asked Joe Rodino. Victor and Gaetano were already out of their chairs and reaching for their handguns.

"I'll g...get it," said Anthony.

"Don't bother," said the man in the doorway. Nobody had heard the door open, not even Anthony. But it had opened, soundlessly, almost of its own will, and suddenly the stranger was standing there. When Anthony shuffled toward the door, out of habit, Victor put his foot out. Anthony fell hard, face-first in front of the stranger, who grinned rather than join in with the laughter of the others.

"S...Sorry," said Anthony.

"Get off the goddamn floor, Anthony," said Joe Rodino. "You look stupid down there."

Anthony scrambled to the back of the room, a dark place where the big standing closet was. The closet was full of clean clothes. Whenever one of Joe Rodino's men got his clothes bloodied from a sloppy hit, the poker room was where he went for a quick change. There was even a small wood-burning stove back there to dispose of any bloody evidence. Anthony looked to see if his own change of clothes, a single white long-sleeved dress shirt, was still hanging there. He'd put it there just the day before. None of the other men had noticed it yet.

"Heard you had a game going," said the stranger, tall and dark and still in shadow. "Thought I'd deal myself in." He was looking straight at Joe Rodino, sizing him up and dismissing what he saw with a quick smirk.

"And just who the hell are you?" asked Joe Rodino.

"Heard you had a game going," said the man again. He stepped into the room and closed the door behind him.

"I *said*, who the hell are you?"

"Thought I might play," said the man.

He took the chair opposite Joe. Anthony stood quietly in the corner. The other two men didn't move.

"I just came to play poker," said the stranger.

"*Did* you?" said Joe Rodino.

"Where you from?" asked Gaetano, speaking out of turn and then regretting it when Joe Rodino shot him a hard look. The stranger didn't look at Gaetano.

"Jersey. Newark."

"And how the hell are things in Jersey?" asked Joe Rodino.

"Okay," said the man.

"Just okay?"

The man didn't answer.

"What was so wrong about staying in Jersey?" Joe asked. He waited for an answer, but not patiently. When Joe Rodino asked you a question, you were expected to respond, and quickly. Anybody in Brooklyn could tell you that.

"I *said*..."

"Nothing much," answered the stranger finally, off-handedly. "Heard there were better pickings over here. Weaker organization. Thought I'd check it out."

"Oh, you did, huh?" Joe Rodino grinned at Victor and Gaetano. "Whatta you know?" he said. "This guy here's gonna take over. Just like that."

"Y...You want a beer, mister?" asked Anthony. "W...We got Ballantine and w...we got Schaefer, too."

"*Shut up, Anthony*," growled Joe Rodino. Then he turned his attention back to the stranger. "I think Big Dom might have somethin' to say about that," he said.

"You'd be wrong there," said the stranger. He smiled past Joe at Anthony, took off the jacket of his summer suit and placed it over the back of his chair. There was a holster under his left arm and a .38 revolver in the holster. He turned again to Joe Rodino. "Well," he asked. "Are we playing poker or not?"

Joe Rodino didn't answer. He was studying the man, considering his options: let him play, don't let him play, or let him play for a while and then kill him. In situations like this, Joe Rodino always leaned toward the latter. "You've got some brass balls comin' in here," said Joe.

"Oh?" said the stranger, his grin widening.

"You got some balls, all right." Then, turning to Victor, he said, "Go ahead. Deal the cards."

Joe reached for the .38 under his left arm and placed it on the table next to him. He challenged the stranger with a look. The stranger followed with his own gun, then pushed it aside.

"It's so noisy here," Anthony said in a soft voice to no one in particular. "I can't think when it's so noisy."

"And cut that shit out!" shouted Joe Rodino.

"It *is* kind of noisy, isn't it?" said the stranger. But, again, he was talking to Joe Rodino. "Must be a big mouth in here somewhere."

"You came here looking for something, huh? Is that it? What makes you think I'm gonna give you *anything?*" said Joe Rodino.

The stranger looked casually at his cards. "You don't have to give me anything," he said. "I was planning to take it."

"How 'bout I give you this?" said Joe, grabbing his .38 from the table and pointing it at the stranger. "How 'bout I do that?"

"Two cards," said the stranger, his expression calm, his eyes gleaming. Victor gave him two cards.

"You think I'm joking?" said Joe Rodino, the gun suddenly heavy in his hand, his grip suddenly weaker. "You think I'm kidding you or something? You come in here, you tell me you're going to take over, just like that, all by yourself, and now you think I'm just joking with the gun?"

"I know you're not joking," said the stranger, his look growing more casual, more indifferent. "But it won't make any difference. Not to me, anyway. Are we playing poker here, or not?"

"I'll goddamn kill you!" shouted Joe Rodino, unaware that he was standing up from the table as he said it. Unaware of the sound his wooden chair made as it tipped over onto the floor behind him.

"Sh...Sure you don't want a beer?" asked Anthony. He was no longer in the shadows. He had moved a few steps closer to the stranger's chair, and no one had noticed.

The stranger calmly lit a cigarette. "I'll bet fifty," he said. "You can either raise, call, or drop. I'd advise you to drop."

"You've sure got balls," said Joe Rodino, picking up his chair and sitting down again.

The stranger matched Joe Rodino's smile with one of his own. His teeth were bright, white, and perfect. His face was perfect also. It had no lines, no creases, no imperfections. It was flawless, god-like.

"B...Beer?" said Anthony, standing over the stranger's shoulder, drooling.

"Shut up, Anthony," said Joe Rodino. "This guy and me, we got business here."

"*Do* we?" said the stranger.

"B...Beer?"

The move was faster than anyone in the room except Anthony had time to comprehend. He had snatched the stranger's .38 from the table with his gloved hand and was smiling across the table at Joe Rodino.

"*Well, will you look at this!*" said Joe, smiling back at his two soldiers and then at Anthony. "*Not bad! Not bad at all!*"

Anthony smiled at Victor and Gaetano. They were putting their guns away. The stranger was still smiling across the table at Joe Rodino. He wasn't speaking.

"Hey, Anthony," said Joe Rodino with a quick laugh. "Shoot the son of a bitch! Go ahead! Shoot him! Pull the trigger!"

"If he even knows how," said Victor, and everybody except Anthony and the stranger laughed.

Anthony seemed to look at Victor and Gaetano for approval. Then he looked casually back at Joe Rodino one last time before putting a .38 slug into Joe's forehead. Just as quickly, he put two bullets into Victor and Gaetano, also in the forehead. As the reverberating echoes of his three bullets rang in his ears, he dropped the .38 on the floor and picked up Joe Rodino's gun. The stranger saw him do it, but he didn't get the full meaning.

"Nice work, kid," said the stranger, getting up from the table. "Looks like the boys in Newark were right about you."

"Looks like," said Anthony in a clear and steady voice. He had stopped drooling. He walked over to the bodies of Victor and Gaetano with firm limbs, examining the bodies, making sure the men were dead.

"I bet you waited a long time for this, didn't you?" said the stranger, picking up his gun from the floor.

"Since I was seven," said Anthony, stone-faced.

"Only one to go now," said the stranger. "Big Dom."

"Yes," said Anthony, half-smiling. "Big Dom."

"Big Dom himself."

"Just one more," said Anthony.

"Where would he be now?"

"He'd be at home."

"We'll get him there, then," said the stranger.

"No. *I'll* get him there. But not today." He pointed Joe Rodino's .38 at the stranger and put five bullets into him. The stranger fell face forward onto the poker table and slid onto the floor.

For a moment, Anthony stopped to admire his work. Then he ambled over to the poker table, past the widening pools of blood. He slipped Joe Rodino's gun into Joe's dead right hand and fired a round into the wall. He did the same with the stranger's hand and his gun, firing the one remaining bullet into the door opposite. He removed his shirt, peppered with gunpowder stains, and tossed it into the stove. The single white glove followed. Anthony put on his clean white dress shirt from the closet, threw a few sheets of old newspaper into the stove, lit a match, and made a fire. When the police arrived, they'd find that the stranger had been shot with Joe Rodino's gun and that Joe and the two others had been shot with the stranger's gun. All very nice and tidy. He practiced his Boris Karloff walk down the long flight of steps to the public phone on the corner, swinging his limp arm as he walked and making sure that several of the passers-by saw him. Then he placed a call to the 76th Precinct station on Union Street and reprised his Boris Karloff walk back up the stairs to the poker room. There he stood by the open door and waited.

"Nice and quiet now," said Anthony, drooling onto his clean white shirt. "Nice and quiet."

The Boy Who Quoted Nietzsche
by Douglas DiNunzio

Richie always sat in the last chair in the last row of study hall. From there he could read his forbidden book in peace and still keep a hawk's eye on Mr. Colavito, the study hall monitor, who sat at a large oak desk at the opposite end of the double classroom. From that strategic position, he could also make sure that none of the other students in study hall -- forty-four mostly honor-student squares -- could not rat on him to Mr. Colavito, who would then be obliged to rat him over to the school principal, Mr. Russell, who would rat him over once again to his parents.

Richie put his weighty tome down just long enough to run a comb through his pompadour and stare dejectedly at his black penny loafers. When he turned one foot enough to see the scuffed bottom, he could still make out the marks where tacks had once held a large metal tap to the heel. Taps weren't allowed in school, nor were jeans. As for cigarettes, he could roll the pack under the sleeve of his T-shirt when he was outside, but he had to keep them out of sight from Mr. Colavito and the honor-student squares. Only a moment earlier he'd realized that his pack of Lucky Strike was in his back pocket, and now he was sitting on it.

He took another quick glance up at Mr. Colavito before picking up his hollowed-out book and starting to read again.

Standing there naked before the mirror, Danielle slowly caressed her large, perfectly shaped breasts and admired the redness of her firm nipples. Waves of silent passion rushed over her. Yes, she was ready now...

Richie liked this one. It didn't have much of a plot, but the title -- *Bad Girl In the City* -- was pretty good, even if the writing was sub-par. The last one he'd concealed inside the hollowed-out book -- the one that said *The Will to Power* on the cover -- was a lot dirtier, but then he couldn't use either of them for a book report in Mr. Weir's English class. School was lousy. It had been lousy ever since seventh grade, and he still had another year to go if he

110

planned to graduate and get himself the hell out of school. He read on.

Now her eager hands slipped quietly, sensually, lower on her young, svelte body. Yes, she had the body that drove men wild, that agonized their desperate loins...

When he next looked up, he noticed that Mr. Colavito was no longer at his large oak desk at the other end of the room. Maybe he'd stepped out for a drink at the water fountain in the hall, or maybe to talk to one of the other teachers who'd wandered by. Mr. Colavito was a gym teacher, so Richie didn't figure him to be one of the brighter bulbs on the faculty. Hell, Richie could probably open a *Playboy* centerfold in his back row seat, and Mr. Colavito would never be the wiser. But he'd had enough visits to the principal's office, enough parent conferences, enough suspensions, so it was best to hide his reading material inside the disemboweled copy of one of his sister's old college textbooks.

Still staring with glazed, rheumy eyes into the mirror, Danielle began to pleasure herself...

"I *thought* so!" roared a stentorian voice behind Richie. A large, athletic arm swept past him and snatched his reading matter from him. All forty-four honor-student squares in study hall turned around. Mr. Colavito was standing just behind him, his middle-linebacker frame casting a sinister shadow across Richie's desk. "Come with me, young man," he said, slamming *The Will to Power* closed and sealing the evidence -- *Bad Girl in the City* -- inside. "Of course, you know where we're going, don't you?"

"Yes," said Richie, forming a frown of disappointment.

"Yes -- *what?*"

"Yes, Mr. Colavito."

Mr. Colavito turned toward the first boy in the first seat in the first row, the one to the right side of Mr. Colavito's desk. "Billy, you are in charge of the room until I return."

"Yes, sir," said Billy, a science nerd and likely valedictorian at graduation time. Richie had beaten him up so many times since sixth grade that it wasn't even fun anymore. Richie couldn't miss the sly, vengeful smile that now took possession of Billy's thin lips. For all those times that he'd spilled the contents of Billy's pocket protector onto the school playground, or in the halls, or in the cafeteria, he had payback coming.

"Class, Billy is in charge now," said Mr. Colavito in his most strident voice, taking Richie by the arm and tightening his grip at the same time. "If there's any nonsense while I'm gone, that person will be making his own little visit to Mr. Russell. Do I make myself clear?"

"Yes, Mr. Colavito," said the forty-four honor-student squares, as Billy, adjusting his thick, plastic-rimmed glasses, grandly took Mr. Colavito's seat behind the large oak desk.

"Oh, not again," said Mr. Russell with sad, tired eyes, as Mr. Colavito pushed Richie ahead of him into the principal's office. Mr. Colavito lifted the heavy tome from under his burly arm, opened it, and placed it on the principal's desk, exposing *Bad Girl in the City* for his enlightenment. Then he stood in the corner by the door, waiting, *enjoying* the waiting. Mr. Russell examined the cheap paperback within the larger, hardbound book, then closed the book so he could read the cover. He left the book closed.

"So, we're reading Nietzsche, are we?" he asked, knowing from past experience that sarcasm had no effect on Richie, but enjoying it all the same.

"Sort of," said Richie, shrugging a bit.

"Sort of, *sir!*" shouted Mr. Colavito from the corner.

"That's all right, Mr. Colavito," Mr. Russell responded with a pleasant smile. "It would be quite nice to see some attempts at civility from young Richie here, but we mustn't expect too much too soon."

"Sort of, sir," said Richie, almost politely.

Mr. Russell looked at Richie. "Where exactly did you happen to come upon *The Will to Power?*"

"My sister's a philosophy major at NYU. It's her book. Well, it *was*, anyway. She's finished with that class...sir."

"And the literature inside it -- the book that you were actually reading? Where did you get that?"

"I'm not at liberty to say, sir," said Richie, finding it easier to say "sir" this time.

"I see," said Mr. Russell. He looked like he might be reaching for the telephone -- another call to Richie's mother at home -- but he picked up the office intercom instead. "Mrs. Wallace, will you bring in Richard Panetti's folder, please." He pressed the button to end the connection and looked for a long moment at Richie.

There was silence in the room before Mrs. Wallace brought the folder in, and a still longer silence while Mr. Russell examined it, tapping his fingers on it several times before looking back at Richie.

"You're a bright young man," he said, his voice still genial. "Your language and vocabulary levels are off the chart on the Iowa Tests that you took in sixth grade. Your grades in elementary school are all exemplary. But, since seventh grade, since junior high, your grades have been poor. You have a D average in Mr. Weir's English class, even though language and vocabulary should be your strengths. You're also failing Dr. Hughes' American History class and Mr. Markot's Spanish II class. You almost failed Latin II last year with Miss Yergin. Your parents, and rightly so, have you in the college preparation program. You're taking Regents courses. So, what's the matter?"

"Mr. Lacey says I'm not college material," said Richie, skipping the word "sir" completely. Mr. Lacey was the guidance counselor.

"Well, your attitude and behavior all seem to point that way, but I don't believe so. There has to be something else going on with you."

"I don't like school," said Richie.

"That is apparent," said Mr. Russell. "Still..." He looked once again at the cover of the disemboweled book. "Have you ever heard of the man who wrote this book, *The Will to Power*? Have you ever heard of Friedrich Nietzsche?"

"My sister drops his name from time to time. Along with some guy named Schopenhauer and another named Hiney."

"That's pronounced 'High-nah,'" said Mr. Russell.

"So?" said Richie.

"They're all great philosophers. Much of what they wrote is still important as a way of understanding ourselves and our place in the world. You would do well to study them."

"Yeah, well, maybe," said Richie.

"I need to return to my study hall," interrupted Mr. Colavito. "The period's almost over." He hovered at the door.

"By all means, Mr. Colavito. I'll see that young Mr. Panetti gets to his next class on time."

Mr. Russell waited until Mr. Colavito had left the office. He took a hard look at Richie, but there was also kindness and patience in his eyes. "You'll try reading one of them, then?" he asked.

"If I say 'yes', you won't tell my parents? About...?"

"I won't, no."

"You promise?"

"Yes, I promise. This will just be between you and me. All right?"

"All right," said Richie.

For the next two weeks, Richie spent his time in study hall doing his assignments. Mr. Colavito watched him carefully from the large oak desk, occasionally slipping out into the hall in an effort to catch Richie once again by surprise via the other door. But there was nothing surreptitious in Richie's behavior to cause Mr. Colavito alarm. Suddenly, Richard Panetti had become a serious student. Suddenly, all was well in study hall.

Until that Friday afternoon of the second week.

Richie had another hardbound book in front of him that wasn't a textbook. He was reading it furtively, looking up every now and then to be sure that Mr. Colavito was not watching him. But halfway through the period, Mr. Colavito ambushed him from behind again, pulling the book from Richie's grip and slamming it closed. They went straight to Mr. Russell's office, Mr. Colavito not even pausing long enough to put Billy in charge.

"Well, he's at it again," said Mr. Colavito, dropping the book hard onto the principal's desk. "See? It's got a phony cover for another book by that guy Nietzsche. *Thus Spake* something."

"*Thus Spake Zarathustra*," said Mr. Russell, smiling calmly.

"That's it," said Mr. Colavito.

Mr. Russell looked at Richie, who was standing resolutely before him, completely without expression.

"He's got another of those dirty books inside," said Mr. Colavito heatedly. "He's ruined another perfectly good book so he could hide one of his dirty books."

"Have you looked inside?" asked Mr. Russell.

"Well, no, but..."

Mr. Russell's eyes fell kindly on Richie. "Well, Richie, are you enjoying Nietzsche?"

"Sort of," said Richie. "This will to power thing, I mean, it sounds okay and all. We need to have some ambition, some drive, if we're gonna succeed, but..."

"Yes?"

"But there's something kind of cockeyed in what Nietzsche's saying about how you use it, like will to power means you don't have to think about being right or wrong when you do something that helps you to push ahead. It's just will to power, and you don't need a conscience or anything. 'Life is simply will to power,' says Nietzsche. But I just don't know about that. It doesn't seem right somehow."

"That's quite astute," said Mr. Russell, casting a quick look at Mr. Colavito before looking at Richie again.

"Well, that's what I got from it, anyway."

"This is one of the better translations," said Mr. Russell, examining the verso, then closing the cover softly.

"I got it at the public library," said Richie. "They've got that guy Schopenhauer, too."

Mr. Colavito was shrinking toward the door as the bell signaled the change of classes.

"Don't worry, Mr. Colavito," said Mr. Russell, noticing his irritation. "I'll see that Richie gets to his next class on time."

"Sorry," said Mr. Colavito in a small voice. He would not look at Richie, who was scowling defiance at him.

"It's an understandable error," said Mr. Russell, and Mr. Colavito left the room. Mr. Russell handed the book back to Richie. "Don't be late bringing it back to the library, or you'll have to pay a fine. Have you almost finished it?"

"Not all of it. It's pretty tough going."

"Well, you can always renew it. Nietzsche isn't exactly a best-selling author, but he's an important one."

"I think I'll try that Schopenhauer guy next," said Richie. "My sister still has her copy of *On the Suffering of the World*. Have you read that one?"

"No, I don't believe I have," said Mr. Russell. "Someday we'll discuss it together, if you don't mind. Of course, I'll have to read it first."

"Me, too," said Richie.

Mr. Colavito never bothered Richie after that. The very next Monday, Richie sat in his familiar seat in the last row at the back of the study hall. A large, hardbound book was propped up in front of him. The cover said: *On the Suffering of the World* by Arthur Schopenhauer. Richie surveyed the study hall with caution for a moment before opening the great tome, following with a look of superiority and scorn. Mr. Colavito was working on his grade book at the large oak desk, almost monk-like in his concentration. All the honor-student squares were similarly engaged at their desks, silent, motionless, meaningless. Richie could not help smiling inwardly as he read:

She lay still, in a kind of sleep. The activity, the orgasm was all his, all his; she could strive for herself no more. Even the tightness of his arms round her, even the intense movement of his body, and the springing of his seed in her, was a kind of sleep, from which she did not begin to rouse till he had finished and lay softly panting against her breast.

"This D. H. Lawrence guy is pretty good," said Richie to himself. "Maybe I'll try that James Joyce next."

Up From Chastity
by Douglas DiNunzio

Miss Mary Holly O'Malley fought back a tear as she dropped a parting red rose onto her mother's coffin. The young priest from St. Finbar's had finished his eulogy, but the casket had not as yet been lowered into place. The fine autumn day offered none of the gloom that her mother would have thought necessary for the occasion. The late Mrs. O'Malley would have preferred rain, a biting wind, and perhaps one or two of the ten plagues from Ancient Egypt to accompany her exit from this life. But then, gloom had been Mrs. O'Malley's response to nearly everything that was important to anyone else.

The graveside gathering at Holy Cross Cemetery had been small: a few neighbors, an elderly aunt and uncle from the Bronx, the nurse who had attended Mrs. O'Malley in her final months, and the corner grocer, Mr. Haller. Mary Holly O'Malley's friend Shirley had been her only comfort at graveside. Both were single, but Shirley had been a married woman in her youth. Mary Holly had been a dedicated spinster, forty-five years old now, and never married. Not even a boyfriend of any consequence along the way. That had been her mother's doing, of course, and even as Mrs. O'Malley was being lowered into a damp and cold eternity, her daughter did not feel entirely free of her.

After the service, Mary Holly and Shirley took the city bus to the Woolworth's on 5th Avenue in Sunset Park. Whenever Mary Holly could find an hour or two free from the demands of her mother, she met had Shirley there for lunch. Shirley worked at Lerner Shops next door, so the Woolworth's was both inexpensive and convenient for her. Lunch dates with Shirley had given Mary Holly the only real free time she'd ever known. Now, of course, Mary Holly had all the time in the world.

What would she do with it?

They took their usual seats at the counter and saw the familiar face of Emmett, the soda jerk. Emmett was fifty-five years old and showing it. Most soda jerks were kids or young army vets back from Korea, but then there was Emmett. Still, he had a kind face, was polite and soft-spoken, and so the two women always felt safe around him. As homely as a girl might be, and they were both so, there was no shortage of mashers in the Borough of Brooklyn. Men whose attempts at social introduction were crude, indiscriminate, and ultimately carnal.

"A tuna sandwich, please, Emmett, and a Coke," said Shirley.

"I'll have the same, please, but go easy on the mayonnaise," said Mary Holly, and Emmett went off to fill the order. It was not quite the noon hour, so the Woolworth's counter was practically empty. A good time for a serious discussion about Mary Holly's future.

"I was talking to Jane the other day," said Shirley. Jane was Shirley's best friend at Lerner Shops. "Jane thinks you should go shopping at Abraham & Strauss, buy yourself a whole new wardrobe."

Mary Holly fairly blushed. "I don't think a new wardrobe would be of much use to an old spinster like me."

"You mustn't think that way," argued Shirley. "Here's your chance to start a whole new life for yourself. Your mother can't tell you what to do anymore."

"Not that she won't try," said Mary Holly with a cynical smile.

"You must banish that thought from your mind," said Shirley. "You're a free woman now."

"Am I?" said Mary Holly, sighing softly. "Well, in any case, a new wardrobe won't nearly be enough."

"So, what *are* your plans?"

Mary Holly cast a surreptitious glance at her friend. Then she scanned the full length of the lunch counter.

"Well," she said in a whisper of a voice, "I have been giving it some thought, and..."

"And?"

"Well, I...you won't tell anyone, will you?"

"Of course not."

"Promise, now."

"Yes, yes, I promise. What, then?"

"Well, I thought I might have a go at fornication."

"Mary Holly O'Malley! Where did you get a mouth like that? Shame on you! And in Woolworth's, too!"

"Well, you *did* ask me," said Mary Holly with no attempt at either a smile or an apology.

"Good Lord!" said Shirley, fairly shouting the words. "Whatever nonsense are you babbling?"

"Shhh," said Mary Holly, putting her index finger to her lips.

Shirley lowered her voice almost to a whisper. "But, honestly now -- *fornication?*"

If anything, Mary Holly's hard, solemn look became even more entrenched. "I'm quite serious, Shirley. Do you know, if I made up a list of the things I haven't done because of Mother, it would be in the hundreds of pages?"

"But *fornication?*"

"And you can add to that a great host of what Mother considered to be vices -- cigarettes, alcohol, lipstick, chewing gum, stockings, high heels, dancing. You haven't been denied those things, Shirley, but I have. Besides, you were a married woman once and should be familiar with the activity commonly known as fornication."

Shirley started to grin, but it quickly turned into a frown. "As an activity, commonly known or otherwise, Mary Holly, I'm afraid that fornication has been somewhat overrated."

"Still, you've done it, and I haven't."

"So, you're wanting to get married, then?"

"Most certainty not."

"Mary Holly, this is *mortal sin* we're talking about here."

Mary Holly's resolve stiffened. "Now, you listen to me, Shirley, and let's face facts. At my age, and the way I look, no one is going to want to marry me. I know that for starters. Mother always thought I should be a nun, and that's what I'm going to do. But not for her reasons, and not before I attempt some other things first. Do you understand?"

"No, Mary Holly, I don't think I do."

"It's all quite laughable, you know, when you think about it. When *I* think about it, anyway. I'm *already* a nun. Don't you see? I've been one my whole life, without ever taking the vows. I've been poor, I've been chaste, and I've been obedient. The good Lord knows I've been all of those things and more...and less. So, before I go off to the convent and become a Bride of Christ, I want to do the things that almost everybody else my age has done. Maybe I'll be over with it in a month, or a week, but I'm going to do it. I've been Mother's house slave all this time, and I want to feel a little taste of freedom, of happiness, no matter how tawdry, before I'm shackled again, and permanently."

"Do you *want* to be a nun?" asked Shirley.

"Not particularly."

"Then, why?"

Emmett arrived with the tuna sandwiches and the Cokes. He pointed to the sandwich that he'd placed in front of Mary Holly. "This here's the one that's easy on the mayo," he said, and smiled. Mary Holly had the feeling he might want to linger, and so she was relieved when someone at the end of the counter asked for service. "Excuse me, ladies," said Emmett, and wandered away.

"Then, why?" repeated Shirley.

"I'm forty-five years old, Shirley. Except for Aunt Helen and Uncle Paul in the Bronx, I have no kin. Who's going to take care of me when I'm an old lady? I have no money, except for father's pension, God rest his soul. If Mother had let me work, even part-time, all these years, maybe I might have made my savings last. Of course, I'm still healthy enough to work now, and I would willingly do so. I am not a slacker. But what about later? What about when I'm old and sick, like Mother was? They'll be nobody to care for me then. In the convent, I'll be safe. I'll be taken care of."

"But, doing that and not wanting it because you want to serve God -- doing it out of convenience -- that's wrong. That's like lying to God."

"He'll forgive me. And he'll forgive all the other things I plan to do as well. He forgives sins, you know. He's good at it, you might say."

"Now, Mary Holly, don't you blaspheme."

"Isn't blaspheming, and fornication isn't a sin anyway. It's not in the Ten Commandments, you know. Not unless you're doing the thing with someone's husband, and I have no intention of doing that. And the other things, they're just vices. You won't go to Hell for smoking or drinking, or wearing lipstick...or dancing, although Mother certainly thought so."

"All right," said Shirley. "And just how do you plan to commit this act of fornication, and who with?"

"Well, of that I'm not quite sure."

"You had best be, and that's a fact."

"Never fear, I will."

"You should get some kind of protection. You can buy them at the drug store. Or have someone buy them for you."

"And why would I need to do that?" asked Mary Holly.

"To prevent disease, of course...and a child."

"Ah, but I've nothing against having a child. Doesn't that go right along with fornication? Isn't that why people fornicate in the first place?"

Shirley suppressed a smile. "Unfortunately, that is hardly why most men engage in the practice. Or half the women I know."

"Well, it's part of the package to me."

"And if you do have a child? What then?"

"I've got that part figured out," said Mary Holly. "There's plenty of couples can't have babies. I'd give it over to some folks if they were good people and could care for it proper. It's like when you make a donation to the Salvation Army. My baby would be a kind of donation. Better to give than receive. That's what the Bible says."

"You're quite mad, you know," said Shirley.

"Be my friend in this," said Mary Holly softly, and stretched out her open hand. Shirley took it.

"Always," she said.

Before going home, Mary Holly stopped at Mr. Haller's grocery. He hadn't come back to work yet after the service, but his clerk Terence was there. Terence was in his early thirties, handsome, and very much the ladies' man. Mary Holly thought about asking *him*, but her tongue got so tangled up inside her mouth that she could barely utter more than a muffled hello and an almost mute goodbye. It was a fine idea in theory, finding a man to fornicate with, but suddenly it seemed so much more difficult to accomplish in practice. Mary Holly had not expected that and had no ready answer for it.

She spent the next several days at home, hoping to find a way around her inaction. There was more than enough to do at first, collecting her mother's things, boxing them up and marking the boxes in anticipation of a trip to the Salvation Army. Then there were the stacks of newspapers in the basement that Mary Holly could sell by the pound to the junk dealer. Her mother had been a pack rat of sorts, and those items would have to go as well, even if they went no further than the trashcan. When that was over, and as she waited for the Salvation Army truck's arrival, Mary Holly found herself doing a great deal of nothing. In the mornings she watched the quiz shows -- *Password*, *Who Do You Trust?*, *Concentration* -- and in the afternoons the soap operas that her mother loved to the point of distraction -- *The Inner Flame, As the World Turns, The Edge of Night*. She sat in her mother's old chair, made her mother's favorite tea, and drank it. She remembered how her mother had spoken directly to the characters in the soaps. "Don't go with that bad man!" she'd say, or "I know what you're up to, and you're not going to get away with it. God will punish you." In the evenings, Mary Holly would pick up *Reader's Digest* and listen to classical music on the old record player. Her mother's records.

"My God. I'm turning into my mother, thought Mary Holly the next morning, and rushed from the house. She had been there for almost a week, all alone, utterly unhappy, and still without a strategy for committing the act of fornication. She went directly to St. Finbar's, and the confessional booth. The priest slid the connecting panel open, and his voice spoke the familiar words: "Do you wish to make a confession?"

It was the young priest from her mother's funeral. For a moment, Mary Holly panicked, but she quickly collected herself and made a somewhat hurried Sign of the Cross. "Bless me, Father, for I have sinned," she said. "It has been one week since my last confession. I have committed the sins of anger, jealousy, and pride. My anger was directed against my neighbor, Mrs. Patterson. She had not closed the covers of her trashcans securely, and cats had spilled their contents into my -- my mother's -- driveway. My jealousy was directed at my friend Shirley, because she has done so many of the things I have never had a chance to do. These were only thoughts, not spoken words, but I know that it is still a sin. My sin of pride seems to be with me always..."

"Do you seek God's help through prayer?"

"Not always."

"You must seek God's help. God will put you on the path."

"I will try, Father."

"Is there anything else you wish to confess?"

Mary Holley paused a moment. She had never been prompted like this in a confessional. Even the priest's voice had a different tone. An accusatorial tone.

"No," she said.

"Are you certain?" Again she paused, and when she answered, she committed again the sin of anger, for there was anger in her voice.

"No," she said. "Absolutely not."

"Very well, then," said the priest. "*Te absolvo.* Now, make your contrition: ten Hail Marys and five Our Fathers. And if you decide that you need my guidance, or that of the Mother Superior, we are always here to help you. Go in peace."

Mary Holly took the long way home. Her mind was troubled, and her mood worsened when she passed people on the street in her neighborhood. People who usually smiled a hello or greeted her by name either turned their heads away or smirked, especially the males. She slammed the front door of her mother's house behind her and pulled down all the window shades. She sat very still for a while, until she started to cry and her body shook.

She waited until five-thirty before calling Shirley. Shirley would be home from work via the city bus. The sin of anger had overcome Mary Holly again, and she knew full well the source of the affliction.

"*You told, didn't you?*" she shouted into the handset. "You were the only one who *knew*. You *told!*"

"I didn't," said Shirley. "I only told Jane. And maybe Emmett."

"*You told Jane?*"

"Well, yes, but..."

"*And do you know where she lives?*" shouted Mary Holly. "*Right here in Bensonhurst. Right here! Two blocks away! Oh, Shirley, how could you?*"

Shirley muttered something else into the telephone, but Mary Holly did not hear it. She had already slammed the handset down. Again, she cried. Not even the convent would take her now. She was doomed to the poorhouse and a life of complete degradation. But then she remembered the story of Mary Magdalene from religious instruction. That fallen woman had been familiar enough with the act of fornication, and yet she was a saint, was she not? And all that Mary Holly had done was *talk* about fornication. Just talk about it, in the abstract, with someone who had once been her best friend and was now a stranger. Yes, it was still possible to find shelter in a convent. Maybe not at St. Finbar's, maybe not here in Brooklyn, but somewhere in a place where no one knew her. Another city, or another state. The thought calmed her. She turned on the record player and played some of her mother's religious music while she read about the most recent unforgettable character in *Reader's Digest.*

When the telephone rang, she picked up the handset without thinking. She heard a stranger's voice, a man's voice. The man said that he'd heard about some job that she wanted done, and he was volunteering to do it. She hung up before he could continue, put *Reader's Digest* aside, turned off the record player, and retreated to her bedroom. For the next two days, she became a prisoner there, a victim of her own shame. *My God*, she thought. *Even the priest had heard about it. How can I even show my face again?* She did not eat, and she did not answer the phone. No, she would never answer the phone again. She would never answer any phone again.

When she finally left the hard cocoon of her bed, she could do little more than sit in her mother's old chair and stare blindly into an empty room. But she would not turn on the television to watch the quiz shows and the soap operas. Nor would she listen to her mother's religious music or read *Reader's Digest*. No, never again. She would put on her best dress and walk brazenly into the liquor store down the street from Mr. Haller's market, where she would buy a bottle of hard whisky and another of gin. Then she would continue on to Mr. Haller's and buy ten packs of chewing gum and five packs of cigarettes, the unfiltered kind. From there she would move on to the drugstore and buy several tubes of lipstick, three pairs of nylons, and those rubbery things that men put over their sex organs -- a whole box of them. On the way home, she would wave that box over her head, as a dare, as a challenge. "*I am Mary Holly O'Malley,*" she would shout, "*and I plan to fornicate for days at a time with the very first man who asks me! What do you say to that, eh? Well? I'm listening, damn you!*"

But then she would break down and cry again.

Late in the afternoon, there was a knock at her door. She ignored the summons, even though it was a polite knocking, a knocking that showed some civility. It continued despite her refusal to answer, a persistent, but not unfriendly, knock. Finally, and with reluctance, she decided to respond.

It was Emmett, the soda jerk from the Woolworth's counter. He was dressed in an inexpensive but well-kept suit that smelled strongly of mothballs. In his quaking hands, he held a bouquet of fresh flowers.

"Oh, no, Emmett. Not you," she said, but quickly apologized when she saw the hurt look in his eyes.

"Well, anyway, these are for you," he said.

"Emmett, whatever you heard, whatever Shirley told you, it was a joke. A very bad joke in very bad taste. I never said those things. Honestly." But then she thought a moment. She was telling a lie. A lie was a sin, and she had sinned enough.

"I know what she said," Emmett explained, "but that's not why I'm here. I don't care about the liquor or the cigarettes...or the fornication. You told Shirley that you also wanted to dance. That's why I'm here. The Knights of Columbus, they've got a dance tonight at St. Finbar's. I know it's short notice. I tried to call earlier, but you didn't answer your phone. I guess that was on account of all the loose talk going around. But anyway, here I am. I know I'm not much. Heck, I'm not even that much of a dancer, but I just kind of like you, that's all. Been meaning to ask you sooner, lots of times, like whenever you sat at the counter at Woolworth's, but I never got the chance. If you were serious about the fornicating –- I mean, if you won't have anything to do with me unless I agree to it –- then I guess I would do that. I think you're a fine woman, in any case, but like I said, that's not why I'm here. If you liked dancing with me and we got to be a regular couple and all, I sure wouldn't mind that. I know I'm at least ten years older than you and not much to look at, but I could be a good provider, too, if it came to that. They offered me a store manager's job a while back at a Woolworth's closer to downtown, but I didn't take it. Didn't figure I needed it, with just me to worry about, but if I had somebody to support, I wouldn't even think twice about taking that job. It's a good job. Plenty of responsibility, a good salary, and I just know that I'd be up to it." Emmett stopped for a moment to gauge Mary Holly's reaction, and he didn't continue his monologue until he

127

saw the smile form on her face. "Well, now," he said, "Just listen to me talk."

"I like listening to you talk," said Mary Holly.

"Does that mean...?"

"It could." And her smile widened.

"I really *don't* care about the fornication part. Honest," said Emmett. "I just want to go dancing with you."

"Can you wait a moment," said Mary Holly. "I just need to put on some nicer clothes and get my wrap."

"I would't mind if you wore lipstick, Mary Holly. Or even nylons. Wouldn't mind it at all."

She started to close the front door, but then she pulled it open again. "Would you like to wait in the parlor while I change?"

"Yes," said Emmett. "I'd like that very much."

O Death!
by Douglas DiNunzio

There was a time when Tom Gant thought that he would never die. It happened to others, of course, and with some regularity, but he did not believe that the scourge was within him. There was no small irony in that belief because he worked at a mortuary on 18th Avenue as an undertaker's assistant. There was a Catholic man on display in the Blue Room, an ancient fellow named Mr. Curry. The Catholics were always blathering about eternal life, but Tom Gant knew that Mr. Curry was just dead. Still, death wouldn't come to *him*. Of that he was certain, and positively so. He was sixteen, his body was in perfect shape, and he had no bad habits. There were, of course, many others his age and younger whom he figured *might* die, and *would* die, such as in automobile accidents, jumps from high places, or gangland rub-outs, but he never took much time or effort to rate their chances. He was mortal, like them, but he simply wasn't going to die like them. He would never even know disease, from which death drew so much of its malevolent strength. No, Tom Gant was going to conquer death. He was going to produce such an aberration in the actuarial tables that those hallowed measurements, those ironclad industry standards, would collapse into chaos, into a death spiral, if you will. Tom Gant was going to live, and live, and then keep on living. That eternal boy, Peter Pan, would have next to nothing on Tom Gant.

Nor was this glorious eternity to be left to chance. He did not eat red meat, he did not use hair products, and he consumed no sugar. Carbonated beverages were avoided at all costs. So were nicotine and caffeine. He would not eat frozen vegetables, especially corn and peas, because he believed that the freezing process corrupted their purity. He kept a good block away, and always upwind, from any source of smoke. A slim cigarette or a factory smokestack, it was all the same to him. Any medicine with an alcohol base was repugnant to him, as were women's fragrances and fumes of any kind other than pure steam. As unhindered sweat was healthy, he would not permit scented antiperspirants under his arms, and he fled from anyone who smelled too strongly of them. He avoided drafts. He did not eat eggs. He avoided touching things in public places, especially doorknobs, without cotton gloves. He shunned dust motes whenever they were visible in otherwise pristine air. He did not pet dogs or cats. He did not sleep on his back. He did not breathe cold air and then warm air. If he got newsprint on his hands, he washed it off immediately. He did not rub his eyes. He did not use a clean handkerchief more than once. He did not wear restrictive underwear. He did not swim in chlorinated pools. He bathed twice daily, and only in a bathtub he had scrubbed down prior to use. He would not write with chalk. He would not brush his teeth with fluoride. He would not wear wool in any form. He would not wear luminous watches. When speaking or being spoken to, he kept a discreet distance of three feet or more. Unless he was speaking, he kept his small, perfect mouth closed. He suppressed yawns, as they permitted miasmas of deathly bacteria to enter the fortress of his body for a longer duration than was acceptable to him. In taking these precautions, Tom Gant was making himself immune from death.

He worked at the mortuary after school and in the evenings. He kept the sidewalk clean outside the building, helped the mortician dress the bodies in clothes provided by their various loved ones, made sure the viewing rooms were clean and tidy, and closed the casket lids when visitation hours were over. He always wore gloves of thin white cotton when at work, and he kept his prudent mouth closed whenever possible. The owner of the establishment, Mr. Guderian, did not question these little eccentricities, because Tom Gant was a good worker and was always on time. Tom Gant felt no need to explain himself to Mr. Guderian, and Mr. Guderian was far too polite to ask questions about his assistant's many eccentricities. Whenever Mr. Guderian asked what the boy wanted to be when he grew up, he gave no answer. To live for an eternity and more, as Tom Gant clearly intended to do, there was more than enough room for multiple professions: tinker, tailor, soldier, spy, grocer, census taker, lawyer, President of the United States. Everything would be changing around him, of course, but he would remain the same. And whenever his few friends or co-workers took notice of his conspicuous timelessness, he would simply provide himself with a fresh identity and move on. To live forever, and beyond forever, required a plan, but a plan was what he had, and the planet possessed infinities of both time and space.

When he saw her for the first time, she was in the Gold Room of the mortuary with her parents. The dearly departed was a woman in her mid-sixties, one of the waxier looking ones. Tom Gant did not know the relationship –– grandmother, neighbor, good friend of the family –– but it did not matter. He was stricken. He was toppled. He was in love. He had never dated, never spoken much to girls unless it was from a distance of three feet or more, but he wanted to speak to this one now. He *must* speak to her now. Even when he smelled perfume and scented soap on her, he had to. Even when he took notice of the unnatural state of her brownish-blonde hair, he had to. A perm was what people called it. A perm involved the use of chemicals. But it was beautiful nonetheless. She was beautiful, even if she wasn't. No one else would call her beautiful. Probably no one before him ever had thought her beautiful, but she was. In his private universe, his tightly guarded infinity, she was. And she was suddenly everything to him. Yes, more than everything. She had noticed him as well, looking away with a coy, subtle smile from the waxen, overly rouged figure in the oak coffin (one of the more expensive ones), and fixing on him compass-like, as intense as a lighthouse beacon, riveted to him, merging with him instantly in that fleeting moment, mind to mind, heart to heart, soul to soul. She smiled at him quickly, he smiled back, but they did not speak. It was somehow enough.

But now there was something else at work within Tom Gant, some new and unwelcome dynamic. For the first time, he felt

Death prodding his formidable defenses, seeking entry, smiling at him wickedly and saying, "See? I'm here."

He saw her write something on a piece of paper and hand it to him on her way out, her parents noticing nothing of it in their self-absorption and their grief. He took the note in his gloved hand, and then, without thinking, removed both gloves to read it. It was an address, written on scented paper. Again, Death smiled at him and said, "Go ahead. Smell it. Isn't it grand?"

He did not scrub out the bathtub that night, did not bathe. He stared almost to the point of blindness at the address. It was a fine one in a fine neighborhood. He wanted to think of her. He wanted to immerse himself in the sweet, warm reverie of her, to swoon gleefully at the very thought of her. But he could not. Death was speaking to him again, and Death was all he could hear. The words were so alien, so threatening, that he could not understand all of them; but he was bound to listen. They told him that his precious immortality was slipping away like a twig in floodwater. He would not live forever if he kept on this way. He would not survive even until tomorrow. He would die, just like all the others. Death was very plain about that. And she would die, too, for she had taken no precautions. Was it fair that Death should take them both for this one regrettable moment of weakness in him? What was a weak moment compared with eternity? And yet, quite suddenly, he could see the lifelessness of the life within that eternity. Yes, he *could* see it now, Death's simple gift, delivered in this moment of despair and confusion. An eternity, yes, but an eternity of loneliness. Loneliness without end, without joy. Without *her*.

"She was nice, wasn't she?" Death whispered as Tom Gant made an effort to sleep.

"Yes," he said.

"You liked her, didn't you?"

"Yes."

"And she liked you."

"Yes."

"It would be a natural life."

"Yes."

"And all you would lose would be…"

"Eternity."

"Endless and meaningless. You see that now, don't you?"

"I suppose. Unless…"

"You can't beat me, you know."

"Can't I?"

"You mustn't try. It upsets the natural order of things."

"But I'm beating you now."

"No, you aren't. You just think you are."

Tom Gant sat suddenly erect in his bed. He glared across his bedroom at the place where he imagined that Death was sitting. Comfortably. Smugly.

"But I *will* beat you. I *will*."

"Not if you consider the consequences."

"I don't care about the consequences. I can beat you."

"It's never been done, you know."

"Jesus did it."

Death let out a howl so raw and raucous that the walls shook. *"Jesus?* Jesus was a *myth!*"

"I can beat you," said Tom Gant.

"She's very pretty, isn't she?"

"No."

"To you she is."

"No."

"You want her."

"No."

"I sent her to you, you know. I can send others."

"Well, send them and be damned!" shouted Tom Gant, his fierce words echoing off the dumb walls. He was out of the bed now, eyes aflame, moving toward the place where his adversary still sat with calm resolve.

And Death smiled.

"The next one will be prettier," said Death. "Much prettier."

"Damn you!" said Tom Gant.

Death watched Tom Gant walk past him to the wooden desk in the corner, by the only window in this small garret of a bedroom. He watched as Tom Gant methodically put on a pair of thin cotton gloves and picked up the scented paper with the address on it. He watched as Tom Gant tore it into pieces.

And Death smiled again.

"I can send another one," said Death. "Maybe tomorrow."

"I'll be ready," said Tom Gant.

"No you won't," said Death, and each of them was certain beyond all certainty that the other was wrong.

CPSIA information can be obtained
at www.ICGtesting.com
Printed in the USA
FSOW02n0138190118
43141FS